J. G. Lockhart

Ancient spanish ballads:

Historical and romantic

J. G. Lockhart

Ancient spanish ballads:
Historical and romantic

ISBN/EAN: 9783744640985

Printed in Europe, USA, Canada, Australia, Japan

Cover: Foto ©Andreas Hilbeck / pixelio.de

More available books at **www.hansebooks.com**

INTRODUCTION

THE intention of this publication is to furnish the English reader with some notion of that old Spanish minstrelsy, which has been preserved in the different *Cancioneros* and *Romanceros* of the sixteenth century. That great mass of popular poetry has never yet received in its own country the attention to which it is entitled. While hundreds of volumes have been written about authors who were, at the best, ingenious imitators of classical or Italian models, not one, of the least critical merit, has been bestowed upon those old and simpler poets who were contented with the native inspirations of Castilian pride. No Spanish Percy, or Ellis, or Ritson, has arisen to perform what no one but a Spaniard can entertain the smallest hope of achieving.

Mr. Bouterwek, in his excellent History of Spanish Literature (Book i, Sect. 1,) complained that no attempt had ever been made even to arrange the old Spanish ballads in anything like chronological order. An ingenious countryman of his own, Mr. Depping, has since, in some measure, supplied this defect. He has arranged the historical ballads according to the chronology of the persons and events which they celebrate; for even this obvious matter had not been attended to by the original Spanish collectors; but he has modestly and judiciously refrained from attempting the chronological arrangement of them as *compositions*; feeling, of course, that no

satisfy any one who is acquainted with the usual style of the *redondilla*
that the ballads of Don Juan Manuel are among the most modern in tl
whole collection.

But indeed, whatever may be the age of the ballads now extant, that tl
Spaniards *had* ballads of the same general character, and on the san
subjects, at a very early period of their national history, is quite certai
In the General Chronicle of Spain, which was compiled in the thirteen
century at the command of Alphonso the Wise, allusions are perpetual
made to the popular songs of the Minstrels, or *Joglares*. Now, it is evide
that the phraseology of compositions handed down orally from one gen
ration to another, must have undergone, in the course of time, a great mai
alterations; yet, in point of fact, the language of by far the greater part
the Historical Ballads in the *Romancero*, does appear to carry the stamp
an antiquity quite as remote as that used by the compilers of the Genei
Chronicle themselves. Nay, some of those very expressions from whi
Mr. Southey would seem to infer that the CHRONICLE OF THE CID is a mo
ancient composition than the GENERAL CHRONICLE OF SPAIN (which last w
written before 1384), are quite of common occurrence in these same balla(
which Mr. Southey considers as of comparatively modern origin.*

All this, however, is a controversy in which few English readers can
expected to take much interest. And, besides, even granting that t
Spanish ballads were composed but a short time before the first *Cancioner*
were published, it would still be certain that they form by far the oldest,
well as largest, collection of popular poetry, properly so called, that is to
found in the literature of any European nation whatever. Had there be
published at London, in the reign of our Henry VIII., a vast collection
English ballads about the wars of the Plantagenets, what illustration a
annotation would not that collection have received long ere now!

How the old Spaniards should have come to be so much more wealthy
this sort of possession than any of their neighbours, it is not very easy
say. They had their taste for warlike song in common with all the oth

* See the Introduction to Mr. Southey's Chronicle of the Cid, p. v.—(Note.)

members of the great Gothic family; and they had a fine climate, affording, of course, more leisure for amusement than could have been enjoyed beneath the rougher sky of the north. The flexibility of their beautiful language, and the extreme simplicity of the versification adopted in their ballads, must, no doubt, have lightened the labour, and may have consequently increased the number of their professional minstrels.

To tell some well-known story of love or heroism in stanzas of four octo-syllabic lines, the second and the fourth terminating in the same rhyme, or in what the musical accompaniment could make to have *some appearance of being the same*—this was all that the art of the Spanish *coplero*, in its most perfect state, ever aspired to. But a line of seven or of six syllables was admitted whenever that suited the *maker* better than one of eight: the stanza itself varied from four to six lines, with equal ease; and, as for the matter of rhyme, it was quite sufficient that the two corresponding syllables contained the same *vowel*.* In a language less abundant in harmonious vocables, such laxity could scarcely have satisfied the ear. But the Spanish is, like the sister Italian, music in itself, though music of a bolder character.

I have spoken of the structure of the *redondillas*, as Spanish writers generally speak of it, when I have said that the stanzas consist of four lines. But a distinguished German antiquary, Mr. Grimm, who published a little *sylva* of Spanish ballads at Vienna in 1815, expresses his opinion that the stanza was composed in reality of two long lines, and that these had subsequently been cut into four, exactly as we know to have been the case in regard to our own old English ballad-stanza. Mr. Grimm, in his small but very elegant collection, prints the Spanish verses in what he thus supposes to have been their original shape; and I have followed his example in the form of the stanza which I have for the most part used.

* For example:—

Y arrastrando luengos lutos
Entraron troynta *fidalgos*
Escuderos de Ximena
Hija del conde *Loçano*.

But, indeed, even this might be dispensed with.

So far as I have been able, I have followed Mr. Depping in the classification of the specimens which follow.

The reader will find placed together at the beginning those ballads which treat of persons and events known in the authentic history of Spain. A few concerning the unfortunate Don Roderick and the Moorish conquest of the eighth century, form the commencement; and the series is carried down, though of course with wide gaps and intervals, yet so as to furnish something like a connected sketch of the gradual progress of the Christian arms, until the surrender of Granada, in the year 1492, and the consequent flight of the last Moorish sovereign from the Peninsula.

Throughout that very extensive body of historical ballads from which these specimens have been selected, there prevails an uniformly high tone of sentiment:—such as might have been expected to distinguish the popular poetry of a nation proud, haughty, free, and engaged in continual warfare against enemies of different faith and manners, but not less proud and not less warlike than themselves. Those petty disputes and dissensions which so long divided the Christian princes, and, consequently, favoured and maintained the power of the formidable enemy whom they all equally hated; those struggles between prince and nobility, which were productive of similar effects after the crowns of Leon and Castile had been united; those domestic tragedies which so often stained the character and weakened the arms of the Spanish kings; in a word, all the principal features of the old Spanish history may be found, more or less distinctly shadowed forth, among the productions of these unflattering minstrels.

Of the language of Spain, as it existed under the reign of the Visigoth kings, we possess no monuments. The laws and the chronicles of the period were equally written in Latin; and although both, in all probability, must have been frequently rendered into more vulgar dialects, no traces of any such versions have survived the many storms and struggles of religious and political dissension, of which this interesting region has since been made the scene. To what precise extent, therefore, the language and literature of the Peninsula felt the influence of that great revolution which subjected the far larger part of her territory to the sway of a Mussulman sceptre, and how much or how little of what we at this hour admire or condemn in the poetry of Portugal, Arragon, Castile, is really not of Spanish, but of Moorish origin—these are matters which have divided all the great writers of literary history, and which we, in truth, have little chance of ever seeing accurately decided. No one, however, who considers of what elements the Christian population of Spain was originally composed, and in what shapes the mind of nations every way kindred to that population was expressed during the middle ages, can have any doubt that great and remarkable influence *was* exerted over Spanish thought and feeling—and, therefore, over Spanish language and poetry—by the influx of those Oriental tribes that occupied, for seven long centuries, the fairest provinces of the Peninsula.

Spain, although of all the countries which owned the authority of the Caliphs she was the most remote from the seat of their empire, appears to have been the very first in point of cultivation ;—her governors having, for at least two centuries, emulated one another in affording every species of encouragement and protection to all those liberal arts and sciences which first flourished at Bagdad under the sway of Haroon Al-Raschid, and his less celebrated, but perhaps still more enlightened son, Al-Mamoun. Beneath the wise and munificent patronage of these rulers, the cities of Spain, within three hundred years after the defeat of King Roderick, had been everywhere penetrated with a spirit of elegance, tastefulness, and philosophy, which afforded the strongest of all possible contrasts to the contemporary condition of the other kingdoms of Europe. At Cordova, Granada, Seville, and many now less considerable towns, colleges and libraries had been founded and endowed in the most splendid manner— where the most exact and the most elegant of sciences were cultivated together with equal zeal. Averroes translated and expounded Aristotle at Cordova; Ben-Zaid and Aboul-Mander wrote histories of their nation at Valencia; Abdel-Maluk set the first example of that most interesting and useful species of writing, by which Moreri and others have since rendered services so important to ourselves; and even an Arabian Encyclopædia was compiled, under the direction of Mohammed-Aba-Abdalla, at Granada. Ibn-el-Beither went forth from Malaga to search through all the mountains and plains of Europe for every thing that might enable him to perfect his favourite sciences of botany and lithology, and his works still remain to excite the admiration of all who are in a condition to comprehend their value. The Jew of Tudela was the worthy successor of Galen and Hippocrates: while chemistry, and other branches of medical science, almost unknown to the ancients, received their first astonishing developments from Al-Rasi and Avicenna. Rhetoric and poetry were not less diligently studied; and, in a word, it would be difficult to point out, in the whole history of the world, a time or a country where the activity of the human intellect was more extensively, or usefully, or gracefully exerted than in Spain, while the Mussulman sceptre yet retained any portion of that vigour which it had originally received from the conduct and heroism of Tarifa.

Although the difference of religion prevented the Moors and their Spanish subjects from ever being completely melted into one people, yet it appears that nothing could, on the whole, be more mild than the conduct of the Moorish government towards the Christian population of the country, during this their splendid period of undisturbed dominion. Their learning and their arts they liberally communicated to all who desired such participation; and the Christian youth studied freely and honourably at the feet of Jewish physicians and Mahommedan philosophers. Communication of studies and acquirements, continued through such a space of years, could not have failed to break down, on both sides, many of the barriers of religious prejudice, and to nourish a spirit of kindliness and charity among the more cultivated portions of either people. The intellect of the Christian Spaniards could not be ungrateful for the rich gifts it was every day receiving from their misbelieving masters; while the benevolence with which instructors ever regard willing disciples, must have tempered in the minds of the Arabs the sentiments of haughty superiority natural to the breasts of conquerors.

By degrees, however, the scattered remnants of unsubdued Visigoths, who had sought and found refuge among the mountains of Asturias and Gallicia, began to gather the strength of numbers and of combination, and the Mussulmen saw different portions of their empire successively wrested from their hands by leaders whose descendants assumed the titles of KINGS in Oviedo and Navarre, and of COUNTS in Castile, Soprarbia, Arragon, and Barcelona. From the time when these principalities were established, till all their strength was united in the persons of Ferdinand and Isabella, a perpetual war may be said to have subsisted between the professors of the two religions; and the natural jealousy of Moorish governors must have gradually, but effectually, diminished the comfort of the Christians who yet lived under their authority. Were we to seek our ideas of the period only from the *events* recorded in its chronicles, we should be led to believe that nothing could be more deep and fervid than the spirit of mutual hostility which prevailed among all the adherents of the opposite faiths: but external events are sometimes not the surest guides to the spirit whether of peoples or of ages, and the ancient popular poetry of Spain may be referred to for proofs, which cannot be considered as either of dubious or of trivial value, that the rage of hostility had not sunk quite so far as might have been imagined into the minds and hearts of very many that were engaged in the conflict.

There is indeed nothing more natural at first sight than to reason in some measure from a nation as it is in our own day, back to what it was a few centuries ago; but nothing could tend to greater mistakes than such a mode of judging applied to the case of Spain. In the erect and high-spirited peasantry of that country we still see the genuine and uncorrupted descendants of their manly forefathers; but in every other part of the population the progress of corruption appears to have been not less powerful than rapid: and the higher we ascend in the scale of society, the more distinct and mortifying is the spectacle of moral not less than of physical deterioration. This universal falling off of men may be traced very easily to an universal falling off in regard to every point of faith and feeling most essential to the formation and preservation of a national character. We have been accustomed to consider the modern Spaniards as the most bigoted, and enslaved, and ignorant of Europeans; but we must not forget that the Spaniards of three centuries back were, in all respects, a very different set of beings. Castile, in the first regulation of her constitution, was as free as any nation needs to be for all the purposes of social security and individual happiness. Her kings were her captains and her judges, the chiefs and the models of a gallant nobility, and the protectors of a manly and independent peasantry: but the authority with which they were invested was guarded by the most accurate limitations; nay—in case they should exceed the boundary of their legal power—the statute-book of the realm itself contained exact rules for the conduct of a constitutional insurrection to recal them to their duty, or to punish them for its desertion. Every order of society had, more or less directly, its representatives in the national council; every Spaniard, of whatever degree, was penetrated with a sense of his own dignity as a freeman—his own nobility as a descendant of the Visigoths. And it is well remarked by an elegant historian of our day,* that, even to this hour, the influence of this happy order of things still continues to be felt in Spain—where manners, and language, and literature, have all received indelibly a stamp of courts, and aristocracy, and proud feeling—which affords a striking contrast to what may be observed in modern Italy, where the only freedom that ever existed had its origin and residence among citizens and merchants.

The civil liberty of the old Spaniards could scarcely have existed so long as it did, in the presence of any feeling so black and noisome as the bigotry of modern Spain; but this was never tried; for down to the time of Charles V. no man has any right to say that the Spaniards were a bigoted people. One of the worst features of their modern bigotry—their extreme and servile subjection to the authority of the Pope—is entirely a-wanting in the picture of their ancient spirit. In the 12th century, the Kings of Arragon were the protectors of the Albigenses; and their Pedro II. himself

* Sismondi's Literature du Midi.

died in 1213, fighting bravely against the red cross, for the caus
tolerance. In 1208, two brothers of the King of Castile left the banner
the Infidels, beneath which they were serving at Tunis, with eight hund
Castilian gentlemen, for the purpose of coming to Italy and assisting
Neapolitans in their resistance to the tyranny of the Pope and Charle
Anjou. In the great schism of the West, as it is called (1378,) Pedro
embraced the party which the Catholic Church regards as schismatic. T
feud was not allayed for more than a hundred years, and Alphonso
was well paid for consenting to lay it aside ; while, down to the t
of Charles V., the whole of the Neapolitan Princes of the House of Arra,
may be said to have lived in a state of open enmity against the Pa
See ;—sometimes excommunicated for generations together – seldom ap
rently—never cordially reconciled. When, finally, Ferdinand the Catho
made his first attempt to introduce the Inquisition into his kingdo
almost the whole nation took up arms to resist him. The Grand Inquisi
was killed, and every one of his creatures was compelled to leave, fo
season, the yet free soil of Arragon.

But the strongest and best proof of the comparative liberality of the
Spaniards is, as I have already said, to be found in their Ballads. Throu
out the far greater part of those compositions, there breathes a cert
spirit of charity and humanity towards those Moorish enemies with wh
the combats of the national heroes are represented. The Spaniards a
the Moors lived together in their villages beneath the calmest of skies, a
surrounded with the most beautiful of landscapes. In spite of their adve
faiths, in spite of their adverse interests, they had much in commo
Loves, and sports, and recreations :—nay, sometimes their haughtiest rec
lections, were in common, and even their heroes were the same. Berna
del Carpio, Fernan Gonzalez, the Cid himself—almost every one of t
favourite heroes of the Spanish nation, had, at some period or other of :
life, fought beneath the standard of the Crescent, and the minstrels of eith
nation might, therefore, in regard to some instances at least, have equ
pride in the celebration of their prowess. The praises which the Ar

poets granted to them in their *Mouwachchah*, or *girdle verses*, were repaid by liberal encomiums on Moorish valour and generosity in Castilian and Arragonese *Redondillas*. Even in the ballads most exclusively devoted to the celebration of feats of Spanish heroism, it is quite common to find some redeeming compliment to the Moors mixed with the strain of exultation. Nay, even in the more remote and ideal chivalries celebrated in the Castilian Ballads, the parts of glory and greatness are almost as frequently attributed to Moors as to Christians;—Calaynos was a name as familiar as Gayferos. At a somewhat later period, when the conquest of Granada had mingled the Spaniards still more effectually with the persons and manners of the Moors, we find the Spanish poets still fonder of celebrating the heroic achievements of their old Saracen rivals; and, without doubt, this their liberality towards the 'Knights of Granada, Gentlemen, albeit Moors,'

> Caballeros Granadinos,
> Aunque Moros hijos d'algo,

must have been very gratifying to the former subjects of 'The Baby King.' It must have counteracted the bigotry of Confessors and Mollahs, and tended to inspire both nations with sentiments of kindness and mutual esteem.

Bernard of Carpio, above all the rest, was the common property and pride of both peoples. Of his all-romantic life, the most romantic incidents belonged equally to both. It was with Moors that he allied himself when he rose up to demand vengeance from King Alphonso for the murder of his father. It was with Moorish brethren in arms that he marched to fight against the Frankish army for the independence of the Spanish soil. It was in front of a half-Leonese, half-Moorish host, that Bernard couched his lance, victorious alike over valour and magic :—

> When Rowland brave and Olivier,
> And every Paladin and Peer
> On Roncesvalles died.

A few ballads, unquestionably of Moorish origin, and apparently rather of the romantic than of the historical class, are given in a section by themselves. The originals are valuable, as monuments of the manners and customs of a most singular race. Composed originally by a Moor or a Spaniard—(it is often very difficult to determine by which of the two)—they were sung in the villages of Andalusia in either language, but to the same tunes, and listened to with equal pleasure by man, woman, and child—Mussulman and Christian. In these strains, whatever other merits or demerits they may possess, we are, at least, presented with a lively picture of the life of the Arabian Spaniard. We see him as he was in reality, 'like steel among weapons—like wax among women'—

> Fuerte qual azero entre armas,
> Y qual cera entre las damas.

There came, indeed, a time when the fondness of the Spaniards for their Moorish Ballads was made matter of reproach ;—but this was not till long after the period when Spanish bravery had won back the last fragments of the Peninsula from Moorish hands. It was thus that a Spanish poet of the after day expressed himself :—

> Vayase con Dios Gazul !
> Lleve el diablo à Celindaxa !
> Y buelvan estas marlotas
> A quien se las dió prestadas !
>
> Que quiero Doña Maria
> Ver baylar à Doña Juana,
> Una gallarda española,
> Que no ay dança mas gallarda :
>
> Y Don Pedro y Don Rodrigo
> Vestir otras mas galanas,
> Ver quien son estos dançantes
> Y conocer estas damas ;
>
> Y el Señor Alcayde quiere
> Saber quien es Abenamar,
> Estos Zegris y Aliataros,
> Aduloes, Zaydes, y Andallas ;

> Y de que repartimianto
> Son Celinda y Guadalara,
> Estos Moros y Estas Moras
> Que en todas las bodas danzan ;
>
> Y por hablarlo mas claro,
> Asm tenguan buena pascua,
> Ha venido à su noticia
> Que ay Cristianos en España.

These sarcasms were not without their answer; for, says another poem in the *Romancero General* :—

> Si es Español Don Rodrigo,
> Español fue el fuerte Andalla ;
> Y sepa el Señor Alcayde
> Que tambien lo es Guadalara.

But the best argument follows :—

> No es culpa si de los Moros
> Los valientes hechos cantan,
> Pues tanto mas resplendecen
> Nuestras celebras hazañas.

The greater part of the Moorish Ballads refer to the period immediately preceding the downfal of the throne of Granada—the amours of that splendid court—the bull-feasts and other spectacles in which its lords and ladies delighted no less than those of the Christian courts of Spain—the bloody feuds of the two great families of the Zegris and the Abencerrages, which contributed so largely to the ruin of the Moorish cause—and the incidents of that last war itself, in which the power of the Mussulman was entirely overthrown by the arms of Ferdinand and Isabella. To some readers it may, perhaps, occur that the part ascribed to Moorish females in these Ballads is not always exactly in the Oriental taste ; but the pictures still extant on the walls of the Alhambra contain abundant proofs how unfair it would be to judge from the manners of any Mussulman nation of our day, of those of the refined and elegant Spanish Moors.

The specimens of which the third and largest section consists, are taken from amongst the vast multitude of miscellaneous and romantic ballads in the old Cancioneros. The subjects of a number of these are derived from the fabulous Chronicle of Turpin; and the Knights of Charlemagne's Round-Table appear in all their gigantic lineaments. But the greater part are formed precisely of the same sort of materials which supplied our own ancient ballad-makers.*

* The reader is referred, for much valuable information concerning the Spanish minstrelsy, to an article on these translations which appeared in the 'Edinburgh Review,' No. 146 :—and which is now known to have been written by Mr. Ford, the learned author of the 'Handbook for Spain.' 1853.

EDINBURGH, 1823.

GRANADA.

CONTENTS.

b

LIST OF ILLUSTRATIONS.

Historical Ballads

THE LAMENTATION OF DON RODERICK

THE LAMENTATION OF DON RODERICK.

[THE treason of Count Julian, and indeed the whole history of King Roderick and the downfal of the Gothic monarchy in Spain, have been so effectually made known to the English reader by Mr. Southey and Sir Walter Scott, that it would be impertinent to say anything of these matters here. The ballad, a version of which follows, appears to be one of the oldest among the great number relating to the Moorish conquest of Spain. One verse of it is quoted, and several parodied, in the Second Part of Don Quixote, in the inimitable chapter of the Puppet-Show :—

'The general rout of the puppets being over, Don Quixote's fury began to abate; and, with a more pacified countenance, turning to the company, Well, now, said he, when all is done, long live knight-errantry; long let it live, I say above all things whatsoever in this world !—Ay, ay, said Master Peter, in a doleful tone—let it live long for me, so I may die; for why should I live so unhappy as to say with King Rodrigo, *Yesterday I was lord of Spain, to-day have not a foot of land I can call mine?* It is not half an hour, nay, scarce a moment, since I had kings and emperors at command. I had horses in abundance, and chests and bags full of fine things; but now you see me a poor, sorry, undone man, quite and clean broke and cast down, and, in short, a mere beggar. What is worst of all, I have lost my ape too, who I am sure, will make me sweat ere I catch him again.']

THE hosts of Don Rodrigo were scattered in dismay,
When lost was the eighth battle, nor heart nor hope had they;
He, when he saw that field was lost, and all his hope was flown,
He turned him from his flying host, and took his way alone.

B 2

His horse was bleeding, blind, and lame—he could no farther go ;
Dismounted, without path or aim, the King stepped to and fro ,
It was a sight of pity to look on Roderick,
For, sore athirst and hungry, he staggered faint and sick.

All stained and strewed with dust and blood, like to some smouldering brand
Plucked from the flame, Rodrigo showed : his sword was in his hand,
But it was hacked into a saw of dark and purple tint ;
His jewelled mail had many a flaw, his helmet many a dint.

He climbed unto a hill-top, the highest he could see—
Thence all about of that wide rout his last long look took he ;
He saw his royal banners, where they lay drenched and torn,
He heard the cry of victory, the Arab's shout of scorn.

He looked for the brave captains that led the hosts of Spain,
But all were fled except the dead, and who could count the slain ?
Where'er his eye could wander, all bloody was the plain,
And, while thus he said, the tears he shed run down his cheeks like rain:—

'Last night I was the King of Spain—to-day no King am I ;
Last night fair castles held my train—to-night where shall I lie ?
Last night a hundred pages did serve me on the knee,—
To-night not one I call mine own :—not one pertains to me.

'Oh, luckless, luckless was the hour, and cursed was the day,
When I was born to have the power of this great seniory !
Unhappy me, that I should see the sun go down to-night !
O Death, why now so slow art thou, why fearest thou to smite ?'

THE PENITENCE OF DON RODERICK.

[THIS ballad also is quoted in Don Quixote. 'And let me tell you
again—(quoth Sancho Panza to the Duchess)—if you don't think fit to give
me an island because I am a fool, I will be so wise as not to care whether
you do or no. It is an old saying, The Devil lurks behind the cross. All
is not gold that glisters. From the tail of the plough Bamba was made
King of Spain; and from his silks and riches was Rodrigo cast to be
devoured by the snakes, if the old ballads say true, and sure they are too
old to tell a lie.—That they are indeed— (said Doña Rodriguez, the old
waiting woman, who listened among the rest)—for I remember, one of the
ballads tells us how Don Rodrigo was shut up alive in a tomb full of toads,
snakes, and lizards; and how, after two days, he was heard to cry out of
the tomb in a loud and doleful voice, *Now they eat me, now they gnaw me,
in the part where I sinned most.* And according to this the gentleman
is in the right in saying he had rather be a poor labourer than a king, to
be gnawed to death by vermin.'
There is a little difference between the text in the Cancionero, and the
copy of the ballad which Doña Rodriguez quotes; but I think the effect
is better when there is only one snake than when the tomb is full of them.

IT was when the King Rodrigo had lost his realm of Spain,
In doleful plight he held his flight o'er Guadelete's plain;
Afar from the fierce Moslem he fain would hide his woe,
And up among the wilderness of mountains he would go.

There lay a shepherd by the rill with all his flock beside him;
He asked him where upon his hill a weary man might hide him.
'Not far,' quoth he, 'within the wood dwells our old Eremite;
He in his holy solitude will hide ye all the night.'

'Good friend,' quoth he, 'I hunger.' 'Alas!' the shepherd said,
'My scrip no more containeth but one little loaf of bread.'
The weary King was thankful, the poor man's loaf he took;
He by him sate, and, while he ate, his tears fell in the brook.

From underneath his garment the King unlocked his chain,
A golden chain with many a link, and the royal ring of Spain;
He gave them to the wondering man, and with heavy steps and slow
He up the wild his way began, to the hermitage to go.

The sun had just descended into the western sea,
And the holy man was sitting in the breeze beneath his tree;
'I come, I come, good father, to beg a boon from thee:
This night within thy hermitage give shelter unto me.'

The old man looked upon the King—he scann'd him o'er and o'er—
He looked with looks of wondering—he marvelled more and more.
With blood and dust distained was the garment that he wore,
And yet in utmost misery a kingly look he bore.

'Who art thou, weary stranger? This path why hast thou ta'en?
'I am Rodrigo;—yesterday men called me King of Spain:
I come to make my penitence within this lonely place;
Good father take thou no offence, for God and Mary's grace.'

The Hermit looked with fearful eye upon Rodrigo's face—
'Son, mercy dwells with the Most High—not hopeless is thy case;
Thus far thou well hast chosen—I to the Lord will pray;
He will reveal what penance may wash thy sin away.'

Now, God us shield! it was revealed that he his bed must make
Within a tomb, and share its gloom with a black and living snake.
Rodrigo bowed his humbled head when God's command he heard,
And with the snake prepared his bed, according to the word.

The holy Hermit waited till the third day was gone—
Then knocked he with his finger upon the cold tombstone;
'Good King, good King,' the Hermit said, 'an answer give to me,
How fares it with thy darksome bed and dismal company?'

'Good father,' said Rodrigo, 'the snake hath touched me not;
Pray for me, holy Hermit—I need thy prayers God wot;
Because the Lord his anger keeps I lie unharmed here;
The sting of earthly vengeance sleeps—a worser pain I fear.'

The Eremite his breast did smite when thus he heard him say;
He turned him to his cell—that night he loud and long did pray
At morning hour he came again—then doleful moans heard he;
From out the tomb the cry did come of gnawing misery.

He spake, and heard Rodrigo's voice; 'O Father Eremite,
He eats me now, he eats me now, I feel the adder's bite;
The part that was most sinning my bedfellow doth rend;
There had my curse beginning, God grant it there may end!'

The holy man made answer in words of hopeful strain;
He bade him trust the body's pang would save the spirit's pain.
Thus died the good Rodrigo, thus died the King of Spain,
Wash'd from offence the spirit hence to God its flight hath ta'en.

THE MARCH OF BERNARDO DEL CARPIO.

[OF Bernardo del Carpio we find little or nothing in the French romances of Charlemagne. He belongs exclusively to Spanish History, or rather perhaps to Spanish Romance. The continence which procured for Alphonso (who succeeded to the precarious throne of the Christians in the Asturias about 795) the epithet of The Chaste, was not universal in his family. By an intrigue with Sancho Diaz, Count of Saldaña, or Saldaña, Doña Ximena, sister of this virtuous Prince, bore a son. Some chroniclers attempt to gloss over this incident, by alleging that a private marriage had taken place between the lovers: but King Alphonso, who was well nigh sainted for living only in platonic union with his wife Bertha, took the scandal greatly to heart. He shut up the peccant Princess in a cloister, and imprisoned her gallant in the castle of Luna, where he caused him to be deprived of sight. Fortunately, his wrath did not extend to the offspring of their stolen affections, Bernardo del Carpio. When the youth had grown up to manhood, Alphonso, according to the Spanish chroniclers, invited the Emperor Charlemagne into Spain, and having neglected to raise up heirs for the kingdom of the Goths in the ordinary manner, he proposed the inheritance of his throne as the price of the alliance of Charles. But the nobility, headed by Bernardo, remonstrated against the King's choice of a successor, and would on no account consent to receive a Frenchman as the heir of their crown. Alphonso himself repented of the invitation he had given to Charlemagne, and when that champion of Christendom came to expel the Moors from Spain, he found the conscientious and chaste Alphonso had united with the infidels against him. An engagement took place in the renowned pass of Roncesvalles, in which the French were defeated, and the celebrated Roland, or Orlando, was slain. The victory was ascribed chiefly to the prowess of Bernardo del Carpio.

The following ballad describes the enthusiasm excited among the Leonese, when Bernardo first raised his standard to oppose the progress of Charlemagne's army.]

WITH three thousand men of Leon, from the city Bernard goes,
To protect the soil Hispanian from the spear of Frankish foes :
From the city which is planted in the midst between the seas,
To preserve the name and glory of old Pelayo's victories.

The peasant hears upon his field the trumpet of the knight—
He quits his team for spear and shield and garniture of might ;
The shepherd hears it 'mid the mist—he flingeth down his crook,
And rushes from the mountain like a tempest troubled brook.

The youth who shows a maiden's chin, whose brows have ne'er been bound
The helmet's heavy ring within, gains manhood from the sound ;
The hoary sire beside the fire forgets his feebleness,
Once more to feel the cap of steel a warrior's ringlets press.

As through the glen his spears did gleam, these soldiers from the hills,
They swelled his host as mountain-stream receives the roaring rills ;
They round his banner flocked in scorn of haughty Charlemagne—
And thus upon their swords are sworn the faithful sons of Spain.

' Free were we born —'tis thus they cry—' though to our King we owe
The homage and the fealty behind his crest to go ;
By God's behest our aid he shares, but God did ne'er command
That we should leave our children heirs of an enslaved land.

' Our breasts are not so timorous, nor are our arms so weak,
Nor are our veins so bloodless, that we our vow should break,
To sell our freedom for the fear of Prince or Paladin ;
At least we'll sell our birthright dear—no bloodless prize they'll win.

'At least King Charles, if God decrees he must be Lord of Spain,
Shall witness that the Leonese were not aroused in vain;
He shall bear witness that we died as lived our sires of old—
Nor only of Numantium's pride shall minstrel tales be told.

'The Lion that hath bathed his paws in seas of Lybian gore,
Shall he not battle for the laws and liberties of yore?
Anointed cravens may give gold to whom it likes them well,
But steadfast heart and spirit bold Alphonso ne'er shall sell.'

THE COMPLAINT OF THE COUNT OF SALDANA.

[This ballad is intended to represent the feelings of Don Sancho, Count of Saldaña,
while imprisoned by King Alphonso, and, as he supposed, neglected and for-
gotten both by his wife, or rather mistress, Doña Ximena, and by his son,
Bernardo del Carpio.]

The Count Don Sancho Diaz, the Signior of Saldane,
Lies weeping in his prison, for he cannot refrain:
King Alphonso and his sister, of both doth he complain,
But most of bold Bernardo, the champion of Spain.

'The weary years I durance brook, how many they have been,
When on these hoary hairs I look may easily be seen;
When they brought me to this castle, my curls were black I ween,
Woe worth the day! they have grown grey these rueful walls between.

'They tell me my Bernardo is the doughtiest lance in Spain,
But if he were my loyal heir, there's blood in every vein
Whereof the voice his heart would hear—his hand would not gainsay;
Though the blood of kings be mixed with mine, it would not have all the sway.

THE COMPLAINT OF THE COUNT OF SALDANA.

Page 10

' Now all the three have scorn of me : unhappy man am I !
They leave me without pity—they leave me here to die.
A stranger's feud, albeit rude, were little dole or care,
But he's my own, both flesh and bone; his scorn is ill to bear.

' From Jailer and from Castellain I hear of hardiment
And chivalry in listed plain on joust and tourney spent
I hear of many a battle in which thy spear is red,
But help from thee comes none to me where I am ill bestead.

' Some villain spot is in thy blood to mar its gentle strain,
Else would it show forth hardihood for him from whom 'twas ta'en ,
Thy hope is young, thy heart is strong, but yet a day may be
When thou shalt weep in dungeon deep, and none thy weeping see.'

THE FUNERAL OF THE COUNT OF SALDANA.

[ACCORDING to the Chronicle, Bernardo, being at last wearied out of all
patience by the cruelty of which his father was the victim, determined to
quit the court of his King and seek an alliance among the Moors. Having
fortified himself in the Castle of Carpio, he made continual incursions into
the territory of Leon, pillaging and plundering wherever he came. The King
at length besieged him in his stronghold; but the defence was so gallant
that there appeared no prospect of success; whereupon many of the gentlemen
in Alphonso's camp entreated the King to offer Bernardo immediate possession
of his father's person, if he would surrender his castle.

Bernardo at once consented; but the King gave orders to have Count Sancho
Diaz taken off instantly in his prison. 'When he was dead, they clothed
him in splendid attire, mounted him on horseback, and so led him towards
Salamanca, where his son was expecting his arrival. As they drew nigh
the city, the King and Bernardo rode out to meet them; and when Bernardo
saw his father approaching he exclaimed—*O God ! is the Count of Saldaña*

indeed coming?—Look where he is, replied the cruel King; *and now go and
greet him whom you so long desired to see.* Bernardo went forward and
took his father's hand to kiss it; but when he felt the dead weight of the
hand, and saw the livid face of the corpse, he cried aloud, and said,—*Ah, Don
San Diaz, in an evil hour didst thou beget me!—Thou art dead, and I have
given my stronghold for thee, and now I have lost all.*']

ALL in the centre of the choir Bernardo's knees are bent;
Before him, for his murdered sire yawns the old monument.
His kinsmen of the Carpio blood are kneeling at his back,
With knightly friends and vassals good, all garbed in weeds of black.

He comes to make the obsequies of a basely-slaughtered man,
And tears are running down from eyes whence ne'er before they run.
His head is bowed upon the stone; his heart, albeit full sore,
Is strong as when in days by-gone he rode o'er Frank and Moor;
And now between his teeth he mutters, that none his words can hear;
And now the voice of wrath he utters in curses loud and clear.

He stoops him o'er his father's shroud, his lips salute the bier;
He communes with the corse aloud, as if none else were near.
His right hand doth his sword unsheath, his left doth pluck his beard;
And while his liegemen held their breath, these were the words they heard:—

'Go up, go up, thou blessed ghost, into the hands of God;
Go, fear not lest revenge be lost, when Carpio's blood hath flowed;
The steel that drank the blood of France, the arm thy foe that shielded,
Still, father, thirsts that burning lance, and still thy son can wield it.'

BERNARDO AT HIS FATHER'S TOMB.

Page 12.

BERNARDO AND ALPHONSO.

[THE incident recorded in this ballad may be supposed to have occurred immediately after the funeral of the Count of Saldaña. As to what was the end
of the knight's history, we are almost left entirely in the dark both by the
Chronicle and by the Romancero. It appears to be intimated that, after his
father's death, he once more 'took service' among the Moors, who are
represented in several of the ballads as accustomed to exchange offices of
courtesy with Bernardo.]

WITH some good ten of his chosen men, Bernardo hath appeared
Before them all in the palace hall, the lying King to beard;
With cap in hand and eye on ground, he came in reverent guise,
But ever and anon he frowned, and flame broke from his eyes.

' A curse upon thee,' cries the King, 'who comest unbid to me;
But what from traitor's blood should spring save traitors like to thee?
His sire, lords, had a traitor's heart; perchance our champion brave
May think it were a pious part to share Don Sancho's grave.'

' Whoever told this tale the King hath rashness to repeat,'
Cries Bernard, 'here my gage I fling before THE LIAR's feet!
No treason was in Sancho's blood—no stain in mine doth lie:
Below the throne what knight will own the coward calumny?

' The blood that I like water shed, when Roland did advance,
By secret traitors hired and led, to make us slaves of France;
The life of King Alphonso I saved at Roncesval—
Your words, Lord King, are recompense abundant for it all.

THE MAIDEN TRIBUTE.

[The reign of King Ramiro was short, but glorious. He had not been many months seated on the throne, when Abderahman, the second of that name, sent a formal embassy to demand payment of an odious and ignominious tribute, which had been agreed to in the days of former and weaker princes, but which, it should seem, had not been exacted by the Moors while such men as Bernardo del Carpio and Alphonso the Great headed the forces of the Christians. This tribute was *a hundred virgins per annum.* King Ramiro refused compliance, and marched to meet the army of Abderahman. The battle was fought near Albayda, (or Alveida), and lasted for two entire days. On the first day, the superior discipline of the Saracen chivalry had nearly accomplished a complete victory, when the approach of night separated the combatants. During the night, Saint Iago stood in a vision before the King, and promised to be with him next morning in the field. Accordingly, the warlike apostle made his appearance, mounted on a milk-white charger, and armed cap-a-pee in radiant mail, like a true knight. The Moors sustained a signal defeat, and the Maiden Tribute was never afterwards paid, although often enough demanded. Such is, in substance, the story as narrated by Mariana, (see Book vii. chap. 13,) who fixes the date of the battle of Alveida in the year 844, being the second year after the accession of King Ramiro.

Mr. Southey observes that there is no mention of this battle of Alveida in the three authors who lived nearest the time; but adds, that the story of Santiago's making his first appearance in *a field of battle* on the Christian side is related at length by King Ramiro himself in a charter granting a perpetual tribute of wine, corn, &c., to the Church of Compostella. Mr. Southey says that the only old ballad he has seen in the Portuguese language is founded upon a story of a Maiden Tribute. See the Notes to his Chronicle of the Cid, p. 377.

THE noble King Ramiro within the chamber sate
One day, with all his barons, in council and debate,
When, without leave or guidance of usher or of groom,
There came a comely maiden into the council-room.

She was a comely maiden—she was surpassing fair;
All loose upon her shoulders hung down her golden hair;
From head to foot her garments were white as white may be;
And while they gazed in silence, thus in the midst spake she.

'Sir King, I crave your pardon, if I have done amiss
In venturing before ye, at such an hour as this;
But I will tell my story, and when my words ye hear,
I look for praise and honour, and no rebuke I fear.

'I know not if I'm bounden to call thee by the name
Of Christian, King Ramiro; for, though thou dost not claim
A heathen realm's allegiance, a heathen sure thou art—
Beneath a Spaniard's mantle thou hidest a Moorish heart.

'For he who gives the Moor-King a hundred maids of Spain,
Each year when in its season the day comes round again—
If he be not a heathen, he swells the heathen's train;
'Twere better burn a kingdom than suffer such disdain.

'If the Moslem must have tribute, make *men* your tribute-money,
Send idle drones to teaze them within their hives of honey;
For when 'tis paid with maidens, from every maid there spring
Some five or six strong soldiers to serve the Moorish King.

'It is but little wisdom to keep our men at home—
They serve but to get damsels, who, when their day is come,
Must go, like all the others, the heathen's bed to sleep in—
In all the rest they're useless, and no wise worth the keeping.

'And if 'tis fear of battle that makes ye bow so low,
And suffer such dishonour from God our Saviour's foe,
I pray you, sirs, take warning—ye'll have as good a fright
If e'er the Spanish damsels arise themselves to right.

''Tis we have manly courage within the breasts of women,
But ye are all hare-hearted, both gentlemen and yeomen.'—
Thus spake that fearless maiden; I wot when she was done,
Uprose the King Ramiro and his nobles every one.

The King called God to witness that, come there weal or wo,
Thenceforth no Maiden Tribute from out Castile should go;
'At least I will do battle on God our Saviour's foe,
And die beneath my banner before I see it so.'

A cry went through the mountains when the proud Moor drew near
And trooping to Ramiro came every Christian spear;
The blessed Saint Iago, they called upon his name :—
That day began our freedom, and wiped away our shame.

THE ESCAPE OF COUNT FERNAN GONZALEZ.

[The story of Fernan Gonzalez is detailed in the *Coronica Antigua de España* with so many romantic circumstances, that certain modern critics have been inclined to consider it as entirely fabulous. Of the main facts recorded, there seems, however, to be no good reason to doubt; and it is quite certain that, from the earliest times, the name of Fernan Gonzalez has been held in the highest honour by the Spaniards themselves of every degree. He lived at the beginning of the tenth century. It was under his rule, according to the chronicles, that Castile first became an independent Christian state, and it was by his exertions that the first foundations were laid of that system of warfare by which the Moorish power in Spain was at last overthrown.

He was so fortunate as to have a wife as heroic as himself, and both in the chronicles, and in the ballads, abundant justice is done to her merits.

She twice rescued Fernan Gonzalez from confinement, at the risk of her own Life. He had asked, or designed to ask her hand in marriage of her father, Garcias, King of Navarre, and was on his way to that prince's court, when he was seized and cast into a dungeon, in consequence of the machinations of his enemy, the Queen of Leon, sister to the King of Navarre. Sancha, the young princess, to whose alliance he had aspired, being informed of the cause of his journey, and of the sufferings to which it had exposed him, determined, at all hazards, to effect his liberation; and having done so, by bribing his jailer, she accompanied his flight to Castile.—Many years after, he fell into an ambush prepared for him by the same implacable enemy, and was again a fast prisoner in Leon. His countess, feigning a pilgrimage to Compostella, obtained leave, in the first place, to pass through the hostile territory, and afterwards, in the course of her progress, to spend one night in the castle where her husband was confined. She exchanged clothes with him; and he was so fortunate as to pass in his disguise through the guards who attended on him—his courageous wife remaining in his place—exactly in the same manner in which the Countess of

Nithsdale effected the escape of her lord from the Tower of London, on 23rd of February, 1715.

There is, as might be supposed, a whole body of old ballads concer[n] the adventures of Fernan Gonzalez. I shall, as a specimen, translate on the shortest—that in which the first of his romantic escapes is described.

They have carried afar into Navarre the great Count of Castile,
And they have bound him sorely, they have bound him hand and hee[l]
The tidings up the mountains go, and down among the valleys,
'To the rescue ! to the rescue, ho !—they have ta'en Fernan Gonzale[s]

A pilgrim knight of Normandy was riding through Navarre,
For Christ his hope he came to cope with the Moorish scymitar ;
To the Alcaydé of the Tower, in secret thus said he,
'These bezaunts fair with thee I'll share, so I this lord may see.'

The Alcaydé was full joyful—he took the gold full soon ;
He brought him to the dungeon, ere the rising of the moon—
He let him out at morning, at the gray light of the prime—
But many words between these lords had passed within that time.

The Norman knight rides swiftly, for he hath made him bowne
To a King that is full joyous, and to a feastful town ;
For there is joy and feasting because that lord is ta'en—
King Garci in his dungeon holds the doughtiest lord in Spain.

The Norman feasts among the guests, but, at the evening tide,
He speaks to Garci's daughter, within her bower, aside ;—
'Now God forgive us, lady, and God his mother dear,
For on a day of sorrow we have been blithe of cheer.

The Moors may well be joyful, but great should be our grief,
For Spain has lost her guardian, when Castile has lost her chief ;
The Moorish host is pouring like a river o'er the land—
Curse on the Christian fetters that bind Gonzalez' hand !

c 2

'Gonzalez loves thee, lady,—he loved thee long ago,
But little is the kindness that for his love you show;
The curse that lies on Cava's * head, it may be shared by thee;—
Arise, let love with love be paid, and set Gonzalez free.'—

The lady answered little, but at the mirk of night,
When all her maids are sleeping, she hath risen and ta'en her flight;
She hath tempted the Alcaydé with her jewels and her gold,
And unto her his prisoner that Jailer false hath sold.

She took Gonzalez by the hand at the dawning of the day,
She said, 'Upon the heath you stand—before you lies your way;
But if I to my father go, alas! what must I do?
My father will be angry—I fain would go with you.'—

He hath kissed the Infanta—he hath kissed her brow and cheek,
And lovingly together the forest-path they seek;
Till in the greenwood hunting they met a lordly priest,
With his bugle at his girdle, and his hawk upon his wrist.

' Now stop! now stop!' the priest he said—(he knew them both right well)—
' Now stop, and pay your ransom, or I your flight will tell;
Now stop, thou fair Infanta, for, if my words you scorn,
I'll give warning to the foresters with the blowing of my horn.'—

　　*　　　　*　　　　*　　　　*　　　　*　　　　*

The base priest's word Gonzalez heard; 'Now, by the rood!' quoth he,
' A hundred deaths I'll suffer, or ere this thing shall be.'—
But in his ear she whispered, she whispered soft and slow,
And to the priest she beckoned within the wood to go.

---

* Caba, or Cava, the unfortunate daughter of Count Julian. No child in
Spain was ever christened by that ominous name after the downfal of the Gothic
kingdom.

It was ill with Count Gonzalez, the fetters pressed his knees ;
Yet as he could he followed within the shady trees ;—
'For help, for help, Gonzalez !—for help,' he hears her cry,
'God aiding, fast I'll hold thee, until my lord come nigh.'

He has come within the thicket—there lay they on the green—
And he has plucked from off the grass the false priest's javelin ;
Firm by the throat she held him bound—down went the weapon sheer
Down through his body to the ground, even as the boar ye spear.

They wrapped him in his mantle, and left him there to bleed,
And all that day they held their way—his palfrey served their need ;
Till to their ears a sound did come, might fill their hearts with dread,
A steady whisper on the breeze, and horsemen's heavy tread.

The Infanta trembled in the wood, but forth the Count did go,
And, gazing wide, a troop descried upon the bridge below ;
'Gramercy !' quoth Gonzalez, 'or else my sight is gone,
Methinks I know the pennon yon sun is shining on.

'Come forth, come forth, Infanta, mine own true men they be—
Come forth, and see my banner, and cry *Castile!* with me ;
My merry men draw near me, I see my pennon shine,
Their swords shine bright, Infanta,—and every blade is thine.'

THE SEVEN HEADS.

[‘It was,’ says Mariana, ‘in the year 986, that the seven most noble brothers, commonly called the infants of Lara, were slain by the treachery of Ruy Velasquez, who was their uncle, for they were the sons of his sister, Doña Sancha. By the father's side, they were sprung from the Counts of Castile, through the Count Don Diego Porcellos, from whose daughter and Nuño Pelchides there came two sons, namely, Nuño Rasura, great-grandfather of the Count Garci Fernandez, and Gustio Gonzalez. The last-named gentleman was father of Gonzalo Gustio, Lord of Salas of Lara ; and his sons were those seven brothers famous in the history of Spain, not more by reason of their deeds of prowess, than of the disastrous death which was their fortune. They were all knighted in the same day by the Count Don Garcia, according to the fashion which prevailed in those days, and more especially in Spain.

‘Now it happened that Ruy Velasquez, Lord of Villaron, celebrated his nuptials in Burgos with Doña Lambra, a lady of very high birth from the country of Briviesca, and, indeed, a cousin-german to the Count Garci Fernandez himself. The feast was splendid, and great was the concourse of principal gentry ; and among others were present the Count Garci Fernandez and those seven brothers, with Gonzalo Gustio, their father.

‘From some trivial occasion, there arose a quarrel between Gonzalez, the youngest of the seven brothers, on the one hand, and a relation of Doña Lambra, by name Alvar Sanchez, on the other, without, however, any very serious consequences at the time. But Doña Lambra conceived herself to have been insulted by the quarrel, and in order to revenge herself, when the seven brothers were come as far as Barvadiello, riding in her train the more to do her honour, she ordered one of her slaves to throw at Gonzalez a wild cucumber soaked in blood, a heavy insult and outrage, according to the then existing customs and opinions of Spain. The slave, having done as he was bid, fled for protection to his lady, Doña Lambra ; but that availed him nothing, for they slew him within the very folds of her garment.

‘Ruy Velasquez, who did not witness these things with his own eyes, no sooner returned, than, filled with wrath on account of this slaughter, and of the insult to his bride, he began to devise how he might avenge himself of the seven brothers.

'With semblances of peace and friendship, he concealed his mortal hatred; and, after a time, Gonzalo Gustio, the father, was sent by him, suspecting nothing, to Cordova. The pretence was to bring certain moneys which had been promised to Ruy Velasquez by the barbarian King, but the true purpose, that he might be put to death at a distance from his own country; for Ruy Velasquez asked the Moor to do this, in letters written in the Arabic tongue, of which Gonzalo was made the bearer. The Moor, however, whether moved to have compassion on the gray hairs of so principal a gentleman, or desirous of at least making a show of humanity, did not slay Gonzalo, but contented himself with imprisoning him. Nor was his durance of the strictest, for a certain sister of the Moorish King found ingress, and held communication with him there; and from that conversation, it is said, sprung Mudara Gonzalez, author and founder of that most noble Spanish lineage of the Manriques.

'But the fierce spirit of Ruy Velasquez was not satisfied with the tribulations of Gonzalo Gustio; he carried his rage still farther. Pretending to make an incursion into the Moorish country, he led into an ambuscade the seven brothers, who had, as yet, conceived no thought of his treacherous intentions. It is true that Nuño Sallido, their grandfather, had cautioned them with many warnings, for he, indeed, suspected the deceit; but it was in vain, for so God willed or permitted. They had some two hundred horsemen with them, of their vassals, but these were nothing against the great host of Moors that set upon them from the ambuscade; and although, when they found how it was, they acquitted themselves like good gentlemen, and slew many, they could accomplish nothing except making the victory dear to their enemies. They were resolved to avoid the shame of captivity, and were all slain, together with their grandfather Sallido. Their heads were sent to Cordova, an agreeable present to that King, but a sight of misery to their aged father, who, being brought into the place where they were, recognized them in spite of the dust and blood with which they were disfigured. It is true, nevertheless, that he derived some benefit therefrom; for the King, out of the compassion which he felt, set him at liberty to depart to his own country.

'Mudara, the son born to Gonzalo (out of wedlock) by the sister of the Moor, when he had attained the age of fourteen years, was prevailed on by his mother to go in search of his father; and he it was that avenged the death of his seven brothers, by slaying with his own hand Ruy Velasquez, the author of that calamity. Doña Lambra likewise, who had been the original cause of all those evils, was stoned to death by him and burnt.

'By this vengeance which he took for the murder of his seven brothers, he so won to himself the good-liking of his father's wife, Doña Sancha, and of all the kindred, that he was received and acknowledged as heir to the signories of his father. Doña Sancha herself adopted him as her son, and the manner of the adoption was thus, not less memorable than rude :—The same day that he was baptised, and stricken knight by Garci Fernandes, Count of Castile, the lady made use of this ceremony :—she drew him within a very wide smock by the sleeve, and thrust his head forth at the neck-band, and then kissing him on the face, delivered him to the family as her own child.   *   *   *   *

'In the cloister of the monastery of Saint Peter of Arlanza they show the sepulchre of Mudara. But concerning the place where his seven brothers were buried there is a dispute between the members of that house and those of the Monastery of Saint Millan at Cogolla.'—(Mariana, Book viii., Chap. 9.)

Such is Mariana's edition of the famous story of the Infants of Lara, a story which, next to the legends of the Cid, and of Bernardo del Carpio, appears to have furnished the most favourite subjects of the old Spanish minstrels.

The ballad, a translation of which follows, relates to a part of the history briefly alluded to by Mariana. In the Chronicle we are informed more minutely that, after the Seven Infants were slain, Almanzor, King of Cordova, invited his prisoner, Gonzalo Gustio, to feast with him in his palace ; but when the Baron of Lara came, in obedience to the royal invitation, he found the heads of his sons set forth in chargers on the table. The old man reproached the King bitterly for the cruelty and baseness of this proceeding, and suddenly snatching a sword from the side of one of the royal attendants, sacrificed to his wrath, ere he could be disarmed and fettered, thirteen of the Moors who surrounded the person of Almanzor.

Forty highly spirited engravings of scenes in this romantic history, by Tempesta, after designs of Otto Van Veen, were published at Antwerp, in 1612.

'Who bears such heart of baseness, a king I'll never call—'
Thus spake Gonzalo Gustos within Almanzor's hall;
To the proud Moor Almanzor, within his kingly hall,
The gray-haired Knight of Lara thus spake before them all :

'In courteous guise, Almanzor, your messenger was sent,
And courteous was the answer with which from me he went ;
For why ?—I thought the word he brought of a knight and of a king,
But false Moor henceforth never me to his feast shall bring.

'Ye bade me to your banquet, and I at your bidding came ;
Accursed be the villany, eternal be the shame—
For ye have brought an old man forth, that he your sport might be
Thank God, I cheat you of your joy—thank God, no tear you see.

'My gallant boys,' quoth Lara, 'it is a heavy sight
These dogs have brought your father to look upon this night ;
Seven gentler boys, nor braver, were never nursed in Spain,
And blood of Moors, God rest your souls, ye shed on her like rain.

'Some currish plot, some trick (God wot !) hath laid you all so low,
Ye died not all together in one fair battle so ;
Not all the misbelievers ever pricked upon yon plain
The seven brave boys of Lara in open field had slain.

'The youngest and the weakest, Gonzalez dear ! wert thou—
Yet well this false Almanzor remembers thee, I trow ;
Oh, well doth he remember how on his helmet rung
Thy fiery mace, Gonzalez ! although thou wert so young.

Thy gallant horse had fallen, and thou hadst mounted thee
Upon a stray one in the field—his own true barb had he;
Oh, hadst thou not pursued his flight upon that runaway,
Ne'er had the caitiff 'scaped that night, to mock thy sire to-day.

' False Moor, I am thy captive thrall; but when thou badest me forth,
To share the banquet in thy hall, I trusted in the worth
Of kingly promise.—Think'st thou not my God will hear my prayer?—
Lord! branchless be (like mine) his tree—yea, branchless, Lord, and bare!'

So prayed the baron in his ire, but when he looked again,
Then burst the sorrow of the sire, and tears ran down like rain;
Wrath no more could check the sorrow of the old and childless man,
And like waters in a furrow, down his cheeks the salt tears ran.

He took their heads up one by one—he kissed them o'er and o'er,
And aye ye saw the tears down run—I wot that grief was sore.
He closed the lids on their dead eyes all with his fingers frail,
And handled all their bloody curls, and kissed their lips so pale.

' Oh, had ye died all by my side upon some famous day,
My fair young men, no weak tears then had washed your blood away!
The trumpet of Castile had drowned the misbelievers' horn,
And the last of all the Lara's line a Gothic spear had borne.'

With that it chanced a Moor drew near, to lead him from the place—
Old Lara stooped him down once more, and kissed Gonzalez' face;
But ere the man observed him, or could his gesture bar,
Sudden he from his side had grasped that Moslem's scymitar.

Oh! swiftly from its scabbard the crooked blade he drew,
And, like some frantic creature, among them all he flew;—
' Where, where is false Almanzor?—back, bastards of Mahoun!'—
And here and there, in his despair, the old man hewed them down.

THE VENGEANCE OF MUDARA

Plate 27

A hundred hands, a hundred brands, are ready in the hall,
But ere they mastered Lara, thirteen of them did fall;
He has sent, I ween, a good thirteen of dogs that spurned his God,
To keep his children company beneath the Moorish sod.

THE VENGEANCE OF MUDARA.

[THIS is another of the many ballads concerning the Infants of Lara. One verse of it—

———El espera que tu diste a los Infantos de Lara !
Aqui moriras traydor enemigo de Donna Sancha,

—is quoted by Sancho Panza, in one of the last chapters of Don Quixote

To the chase goes Rodrigo with hound and with hawk;
But what game he desires is revealed in his talk:
'Oh, in vain have I slaughtered the Infants of Lara:
There's an heir in his hall—there's the bastard Mudara—
There's the son of the renegade—spawn of Mahoun—
If I meet with Mudara, my spear brings him down.'

While Rodrigo rides on in the heat of his wrath,
A stripling, armed cap-a-pee, crosses his path:
'Good morrow, young esquire.'—'Good morrow, old knight.'—
'Will you ride with our party, and share our delight?'—
'Speak your name, courteous stranger,' the stripling replied;
'Speak your name and your lineage, ere with you I ride.'—

'My name is Rodrigo,' thus answered the knight;
'Of the line of old Lara, though barred from my right,

For the kinsman of Salas proclaims for the heir
Of our ancestor's castles and forestries fair,
A bastard, a renegade's offspring—Mudara—
Whom I'll send, if I can, to the Infants of Lara.'—

' I behold thee, disgrace to thy lineage !—with joy,
' I behold thee, thou murderer !' answered the boy—
' The bastard you curse, you behold him in me ;
But his brothers' avenger that bastard shall be !
Draw ! for I am the renegade's offspring, Mudara—
We shall see who inherits the life-blood of Lara ! '

' I am armed for the forest-chase—not for the fight ;
Let me go for my shield and my sword,' cries the knight ;—
' Now the mercy you dealt to my brothers of old,
Be the hope of that mercy the comfort you hold ;
Die, foeman to Sancha—die, traitor to Lara ! '—
As he spake, there was blood on the spear of Mudara.

THE WEDDING OF THE LADY THERESA.

[THE following passage occurs in Mariana's History (Book viii. Chap. 5 : –)
' There are who affirm that this Moor's name was Abdalla, and that he had
to wife Doña Theresa, sister to Alphonso, King of Leon, with consent of
that prince. Great and flagrant dishonour ! The purpose was to gain
new strength to his kingdom by this Moorish alliance ; but some pretences
were set forth that Abdalla had exhibited certain signs of desiring to be a
Christian, that in a short time he was to be baptised, and the like.

' The Lady Theresa, deceived with these representations, was con-
ducted to Toledo, where the nuptials were celebrated in great splendour,

with games and sports, and a banquet, which lasted until night.   The
company having left the tables, the bride was then carried to bed; but
when the amorous Moor drew near to her—'Away,' said she; 'let
such heavy calamity, such baseness, be far from me!   One of two things
must be—either be baptized, thou with thy people, and then come to my
arms, or, refusing to do so, keep away from me for ever.   If otherwise,
fear the vengeance of men, who will not overlook my insult and suffering;
and the wrath of God, above all, which will follow the violation of a
Christian lady's chastity.   Take good heed, and let not luxury, that
smooth pest, be thy ruin.'   But the Moor took no heed of her words, and
lay with her against her will.   The Divine vengeance followed swiftly, for
there fell on him a severe malady, and he well knew within himself from
what cause it arose.   Immediately he sent back Doña Theresa to her
brother's house, with great gifts which he had bestowed on her; but she
made herself a nun, in the Convent of Las Huelgas (near Burgos,) and
there passed the remainder of her days in pious labours and devotions, in
which she found her consolation for the outrage which had been committed
on her.'

 The ballad of which a translation follows, tells the same story :—
  En los reynos de Leon el quinto Alfonso roynava, &c.]

'Twas when the fifth Alphonso in Leon held his sway,
King Abdallah of Toledo an embassy did send ;
He asked his sister for a wife, and in an evil day
Alphonso sent her, for he feared Abdallah to offend ;
He feared to move his anger, for many times before
He had received in danger much succour from the Moor.

Sad heart had fair Theresa when she their paction know ;
With streaming tears she heard them tell she 'mong the Moors must go ;
That she, a Christian damosell, a Christian firm and true,
Must wed a Moorish husband, it well might cause her wo ;
But all her tears and all her prayers they are of small avail ;
At length she for her fate prepares, a victim sad and pale.

The King hath sent his sister to fair Toledo town.
Where then the Moor Abdallah his royal state did keep ;
When she drew near, the Moslem from his golden throne came down.
And courteously received her, and bade her cease to weep ;
With loving words he pressed her to come his bower within ;
With kisses he caressed her, but still she feared the sin.

'Sir King, Sir King, I pray thee'—'twas thus Theresa spake—
'I pray thee have compassion, and do to me no wrong ;
For sleep with thee I may not, unless the vows I break
Whereby I to the holy church of Christ my Lord belong ;
But thou hast sworn to serve Mahoun, and if this thing should be.
The curse of God it must bring down upon thy realm and thee.

'The angel of Christ Jesu, to whom my heavenly Lord
Hath given my soul in keeping, is ever by my side ;
If thou dost me dishonour, he will unsheath his sword,
And smite thy body fiercely, at the crying of thy bride.
Invisible he standeth ; his sword, like fiery flame,
Will penetrate thy bosom, the hour that sees my shame.'—

The Moslem heard her with a smile ; the earnest words she said
He took for bashful maiden's wile, and drew her to his bower.
In vain Theresa prayed and strove—she pressed Abdallah's bed,
Perforce received his kiss of love, and lost her maiden flower.
A woful woman there she lay, a loving lord beside,
And earnestly to God did pray her succour to provide.

.The Angel of Christ Jesu her sore complaint did hear,
And plucked his heavenly weapon from out his sheath unseen ;
He waved the brand in his right hand, and to the King came near,
And drew the point o'er limb and joint, beside the weeping Queen.
A mortal weakness from the stroke upon the King did fall :—
He could not stand when daylight broke, but on his knees must crawl.

THE YOUNG CID

Abdalla shuddered inly, when he this sickness felt,
And called upon his barons, his pillow to come nigh ;
' Rise up,' he said, ' my liegemen,' as round his bed they knelt,
' And take this Christian lady, else certainly I die ;
Let gold be in your girdles, and precious stones beside,
And swiftly ride to Leon, and render up my bride.'—

When they were come to Leon, Theresa would not go
Into her brother's dwelling, where her maiden years were spent ;
But o'er her downcast visage a white veil she did throw,
And to the ancient nunnery of Las Huelgas went.
There long, from worldly eyes retired, a holy life she led ;
There she, an aged saint, expired—there sleeps she with the dead.

THE YOUNG CID.

[THE ballads in the collection of Escobar, entitled *Romancero e Historia del muy valeroso Cavallero El Cid Ruy Diaz de Bivar*, are said by Mr. Southey to be in general possessed of but little merit Notwithstanding the opinion of that great scholar and poet, I have had much pleasure in reading them ; and have translated a very few, which may serve, perhaps, as a sufficient specimen. The following is a version of that which stands fifth in Escobar :—

*   Cavalga Diogo Laynez al buen Rey besar la mano, &c.*]

Now rides Diego Laynez to kiss the good King's hand ;
Three hundred men of gentry go with him from his land ;
Among them, young Rodrigo, the proud Knight of Bivar ;
The rest on mules are mounted, he on his horse of war.

They ride in glittering gowns of soye—he harnessed like a lord ;
There is no gold about the boy, but the crosslet of his sword ;
The rest have gloves of sweet perfume—he gauntlets strong of mail ;
They broidered cap and flaunting plume—he crest untaught to quail.

All talking with each other thus along their way they passed,
But now they've come to Burgos, and met the King at last ;
When they came near his nobles, a whisper through them ran—
'He rides amidst the gentry that slew the Count Lozan.'

With very haughty gesture Rodrigo reined his horse,
Right scornfully he shouted, when he heard them so discourse ;—
'If any of his kinsmen or vassals dare appear,
The man to give them answer, on horse or foot, is here.'—

'The devil ask the question !' thus muttered all the band :—
With that they all alighted, to kiss the good King's hand,
All but the proud Rodrigo—he in his saddle stayed—
Then turned to him his father (you may hear the words he said.)

'Now, 'light, my son, I pray thee, and kiss the good King's hand,
He is our Lord, Rodrigo—we hold of him our land.'—
But when Rodrigo heard him, he looked in sulky sort—
I wot the words he answered, they were both cold and short.

'Had any other said it, his pains had well been paid,
But thou, sir, art my father, thy word must be obeyed.'—
With that he sprung down lightly, before the King to kneel,
But as the knee was bending, out leapt his blade of steel.

The King drew back in terror, when he saw the sword was bare:
'Stand back, stand back, Rodrigo ! in the devil's name, beware !
Your looks bespeak a creature of father Adam's mould,
But in your wild behaviour you're like some lion bold.'

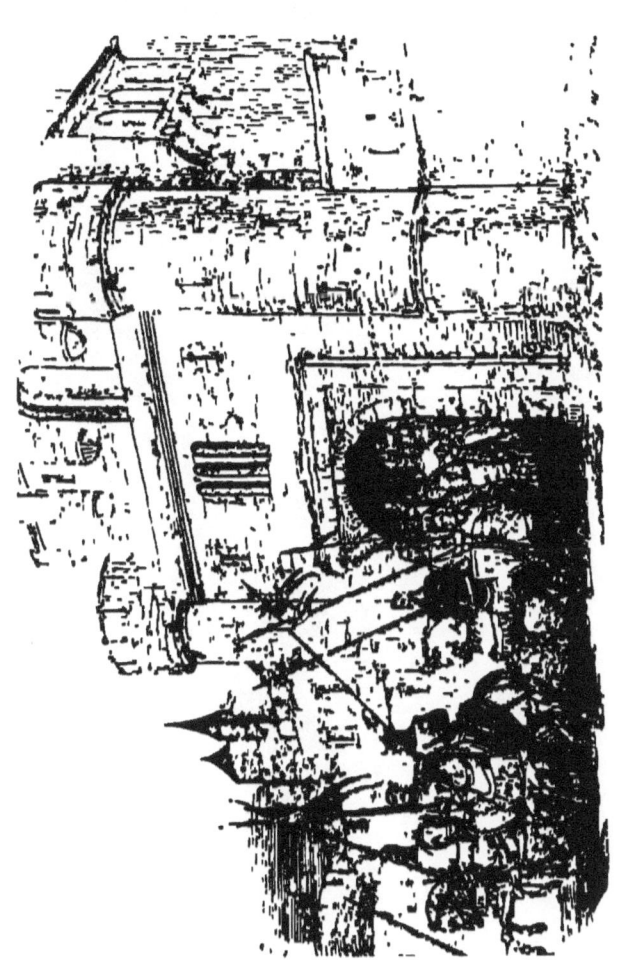

THE GATE OF BURGOS

Page 61

When Rodrigo heard him say so, he leapt into his seat,
And thence he made his answer, with visage nothing sweet :—
' I'd think it little honor to kiss a kingly palm,
And if my father's kissed it, thereof ashamed I am.'—

When he these words had uttered, he turned him from the gate—
His true three hundred gentles behind him followed straight ;
If with good gowns they came that day, with better arms they went,
And if their mules behind did stay, with horses they're content.

XIMENA DEMANDS VENGEANCE.

[This ballad represents Ximena Gomez as, in person, demanding of the King
    vengeance for the death of her father, whom the young Rodrigo de Bivar
    had fought and slain.

                Grande rumor se levanta
                De gritos, armas, y vozes,
                En el Palacio de Burgos
                Donde son los buenos homes, &c.]

Within the court at Burgos a clamour doth arise,
Of arms on armour clashing, of screams, and shouts, and cries ,
The good men of the King, that sit his hall around,
All suddenly upspring, astonished at the sound.

The King leans from his chamber, from the balcony on high :
' What means this furious clamour my palace-porch so nigh ?
But when he looked below him, there were horsemen at the gate,
And the fair Ximena Gomez, kneeling in woful state.

                                                        D

Upon her neck, disordered, hung down the lady's hair,
And floods of tears were streaming upon her bosom fair;
Sore wept she for her father, the Count that had been slain:
Loud cursed she Rodrigo, whose sword his blood did stain.

They turned to bold Rodrigo, I wot his cheek was red;
With haughty wrath he listened to the words Ximena said:
'Good King, I cry for justice.   Now, as my voice thou hearest,
So God befriend the children that in thy land thou rearest.

'The King that doth not justice hath forfeited his claim
Both to his kingly station and to his knightly name;
He should not sit at banquet, clad in the royal pall,
Nor should the nobles serve him on knee within the hall.

'Good King, I am descended from barons bright of old,
Who with Castilian pennons Pelayo did uphold;
But if my strain were lowly, as it is high and clear,
Thou still shouldst prop the feeble, and the afflicted hear.

'For thee, fierce homicide! draw, draw thy sword once more,
And pierce the breast which wide I spread thy stroke before;
Because I am a woman, my life thou need'st not spare:
I am Ximena Gomez, my slaughtered father's heir.

'Since thou hast slain the knight that did our faith defend,
And still to shameful flight all the Almanzors send,
'Tis but a little matter that I confront thee so:
Come, traitor, slay his daughter—she needs must be thy foe.'

Ximena gazed upon him, but no reply could meet;
His fingers held the bridle, he vaulted to his seat.
She turned her to the nobles, I wot her cry was loud,
But not a man durst follow; slow rode he through the crowd.

THE CID AND THE FIVE MOORISH KINGS.

[THE reader will find the story of this ballad in Mr. Southey's chronicle (Book i.,
Sect. 4.) 'And the Moors entered Castile in great power, for there came
with them five kings,' &c]

WITH fire and desolation the Moors are in Castile,
Five Moorish kings together, and all their vassals leal ;
They've passed in front of Burgos, through the Oca-Hills they've run,
They've plundered Belforado, San Domingo's harm is done.

In Najara and Logrono there's waste and disarray :—
And now with Christian captives, a very heavy prey,
With many men and women, and boys and girls beside,
In joy and exultation to their own realms they ride.

For neither king nor noble would dare their path to cross,
Until the good Rodrigo heard of this skaith and loss ;
In old Bivar the castle he heard the tidings told—
(He was as yet a stripling, not twenty summers old).

He mounted Bavieca, his friends he with him took,
He raised the country round him, no more such scorn to brook :
He rode to the hills of Oca, where then the Moormen lay,
He conquered all the Moormen, and took from them their prey.

To every man had mounted he gave his part of gain,
Dispersing the much treasure the Saracens had ta'en ;
The kings wore all the booty himself had from the war,
Them led he to the castle, his stronghold of Bivar.

D 2

He brought them to his mother, proud dame that day was she:—
They owned him for their Signior, and then he set them free;
Home went they, much commending Rodrigo of Bivar,
And sent him lordly tribute from their Moorish realms afar.

THE CID'S COURTSHIP.

[See Mr. Southey's Chronicle (Book 1, Sect. 5.) for this part of the Cid's
story, as given in the General Chronicle of Spain.]

Now, of Rodrigo de Bivar great was the fame that ran,
How he five kings had vanquished, proud Moormen every one;
And how, when they consented to hold of him their ground,
He freed them from the prison wherein they had been bound.

To the good King Fernando, in Burgos where he lay,
Came then Ximena Gomez, and thus to him did say:—
'I am Don Gomez' daughter, in Gormaz Count was he;
Him slew Rodrigo of Bivar in battle valiantly.

'Now am I come before you, this day a boon to crave—
And it is that I to husband may this Rodrigo have;
Grant this, and I shall hold me a happy damoscll,
Much honored shall I hold me—I shall be married well.

'I know he's born for thriving, none like him in the land;
I know that none in battle against his spear may stand;
Forgiveness is well pleasing in God our Saviour's view,
And I forgive him freely, for that my sire he slew.'

Right pleasing to Fernando was the thing she did propose;
He writes his letter swiftly, and forth his foot-page goes;
I wot, when young Rodrigo saw how the king did write,
He leapt on Bavieca—I wot his leap was light.

With his own troop of true men forthwith he took the way,
Three hundred friends and kinsmen, all gently born were they;
All in one color mantled, in armor gleaming gay,
New were both scarf and scabbard, when they went forth that day.

The King came out to meet him, with words of hearty cheer;
Quoth he, 'My good Rodrigo, right welcome art thou here;
This girl Ximena Gomez would have thee for her lord,
Already for the slaughter her grace she doth accord.

'I pray thee be consenting—my gladness will be great;
Thou shalt have lands in plenty to strengthen thine estate.'
'Lord King,' Rodrigo answers, 'in this and all beside,
Command, and I'll obey thee.   The girl shall be my bride!'

But when the fair Ximena came forth to plight her hand,
Rodrigo, gazing on her, his face could not command:
He stood and blushed before her;—thus at the last said he -
'I slew thy sire, Ximena, but not in villany:

'In no disguise I slew him—man against man I stood;
There was some wrong between us, and I did shed his blood.
I slew a man, I owe a man; fair lady, by God's grace!
An honored husband thou shalt have in thy dead father's place.

THE CID'S WEDDING.

[THE following ballad, which contains some curious traits of rough antique manners, is not included in Escobar's collection. There is one there descriptive of the same event, but apparently executed by a much more modern hand.]

WITHIN his hall of Burgos the King prepares the feast ;
He makes his preparation for many a noble guest.
It is a joyful city, it is a gallant day,
'Tis the Campeador's wedding, and who will bide away ?

Layn Calvo, the Lord Bishop, he first comes forth the gate ;
Behind him comes Ruy Diaz, in all his bridal state ;
The crowd makes way before them as up the street they go ;
For the multitude of people their steps must needs be slow.

The King had taken order that they should rear an arch,
From house to house all over, in the way that they must march ;
They have hung it all with lances, and shields, and glittering helms,
Brought by the Campeador from out the Moorish realms.

They have scattered olive branches and rushes on the street,
And the ladies fling down garlands at the Campeador's feet ;
With tapestry and broidery their balconies between,
To do his bridal honor, their walls the burghers screen.

They lead the bulls before them all covered o'er with trappings;
The little boys pursue them with hootings and with clappings;
The fool, with cap and bladder, upon his ass goes prancing,
Amidst troops of captive maidons with bells and cymbals dancing.

With antics and with fooleries, with shouting and with laughter,
They fill the streets of Burgos—and The Devil he comes after;
For the King has hired the horned fiend for twenty maravedis,
And there he goes, with hoofs for toes, to terrify the ladies.

Then comes the bride Ximena—the King he holds her hand;
And the Queen; and, all in fur and pall, the nobles of the land.
All down the street the cars of wheat are round Ximena flying,
But the King lifts off her bosom sweet whatever there is lying.

Quoth Suero, when he saw it, (his thought you understand,)
' 'Tis a fine thing to be a King—but Heaven make me a Hand ! '
The King was very merry, when he was told of this,
And swore the bride, ere eventide, must give the boy a kiss.

The King went always talking, but she held down her head,
And seldom gave an answer to any thing he said;
It was better to be silent, among such a crowd of folk,
Than utter words so meaningless as she did when she spoke.

THE CID AND THE LEPER.

[Like our own Robert the Bruce, the great Spanish hero is represented as exhibiting on many occasions, great gentleness of disposition and compassion. But while old Barbour is contented with such simple anecdotes as that of a poor laundress being suddenly taken ill with the pains of child-birth, and the King stopping the march of his army rather than leave her unprotected, the minstrels of Spain, never losing an opportunity of gratifying the superstitious propensities of their audience, are sure to let no similar incident in their champion's history pass without a miracle.]

He has ta'en some twenty gentlemen, along with him to go,
For he will pay that ancient vow he to Saint James doth owe :
To Compostella, where the shrine doth by the altar stand,
The good Rodrigo de Bivar is riding through the land.

Whore'er he goes, much alms he throws, to feeble folk and poor ;
Beside the way for him they pray, him blessings to procure ;
For, God and Mary Mother, their heavenly grace to win,
His hand was ever bountiful : great was his joy therein.

And there, in middle of the path, a leper did appear ;
In a deep slough the leper lay ; to help would none come near,
Though earnestly he thence did cry, ' For God our Saviour's sake,
From out this fearful jeopardy a Christian brother take.'

When Roderick heard that piteous word, he from his horse came down ;
For all they said, no stay he made, that noble champioun ;
He reached his hand to pluck him forth, of fear was no account,
Then mounted on his steed of worth, and made the leper mount.

Behind him rode the leprous man; when to their hostelrie
They came, he made him eat with him at table cheerfully;
While all the rest from that poor guest with loathing shrunk away,
To his own bed the wretch he led—beside him there he lay.

All at the mid-hour of the night, while good Rodrigo slept,
A breath came from the leprosito, which through his shoulders crept;
Right through the body, by the heart, passed forth that breathing cold;
I wot he leaped up with a start, in terrors manifold.

He groped for him in the bed, but him he could not find,
Through the dark chamber groped he with very anxious mind;
Loudly he lifted up his voice, with speed a lamp was brought,
Yet nowhere was the leper seen, though far and near they sought.

He turned him to his chamber, God wot! perplexed sore
With that which had befallen—when lo! his face before
There stood a man all clothed in vesture shining white:
Thus said the vision, 'Sleepest thou, or wakest thou, Sir Knight?

'I sleep not,' quoth Rodrigo; 'but tell me who art thou,
For, in the midst of darkness, much light is on thy brow?'
'I am the holy Lazarus—I come to speak with thee;
I am the same poor leper thou savedst for charity.

'Not vain the trial, nor in vain thy victory hath been;
God favors thee, for that my pain thou didst relieve yestreen.
There shall be honor with thee, in battle and in peace,
Success in all thy doings, and plentiful increase.

'Strong enemies shall not prevail thy greatness to undo;
Thy name shall make men's cheeks full pale—Christians and Moslem too;
A death of honor shalt thou die, such grace to thee is given,
Thy soul shall part victoriously, and be received in heaven.'

When he these gracious words had said, the spirit vanished quite.
Rodrigo rose and knelt him down—he knelt till morning light;
Unto the heavenly Father, and Mary Mother dear,
He made his prayer right humbly, till dawned the morning clear.

BAVIECA.

[MONTAIGNE, in his curious Essay, entitled 'Des Destriers' says that all the world knows every thing about Bucephalus. The name of the favourite charger of the Cid Ruy Diaz is scarcely less celebrated Notice is taken of him in almost every one of the hundred ballads concerning the history of his master—and there are some among them, of which the horse is more truly the hero than his rider. In one of these ballads, the Cid in giving directions about his funeral; he desires that they shall place his body 'in full armour upon Bavieca,' and so conduct him to the church of San Pedro de Cardeña. This was done accordingly; and, says another ballad:—

> Truxeron pues a Babieca;
> Y en mirandolo se puso
> Tan triste como si fuera
> Mas rasonable que bruto.

In the Cid's last will, mention is also made of his noble charger. 'When ye bury Bavieca, dig deep,' says Ruy Diaz; 'for shameful thing were it that he should be eaten by curs, who hath trampled down so much currish flesh of Moors.' He was buried near his master, under the trees in front of the convent of San Pedro of Cardeña.]

THE King looked on him kindly, as on a vassal true;
Then to the King Ruy Diaz spake after reverence due—
'O King, the thing is shameful, that any man beside
The liege lord of Castile himself should Bavieca ride:

'For neither Spain nor Araby could another charger bring
So good as he, and certes, the best befits my king.
But that you may behold him, and know him to the core,
I'll make him go as he was wont when his nostrils smelt the Moor.

With that, the Cid, clad as he was in mantle furred and wide,
On Bavieca vaulting, put the rowel in his side ;
And up and down, and round and round, so fierce was his career,
Streamed like a pennon on the wind Ruy Diaz' minivere.

And all that saw them praised them—they lauded man and horse,
As matched well, and rivalless for gallantry and force ;
Ne'er had they looked on horseman might to this knight come near,
Nor on other charger worthy of such a cavalier.

Thus, to and fro a-rushing, the fierce and furious steed,
He snapped in twain his hither rein—'God pity now the Cid !—
God pity Diaz !' cried the Lords—but when they looked again,
They saw Ruy Diaz ruling him with the fragment of his rein ;
They saw him proudly ruling with gesture firm and calm,
Like a true lord commanding—and obeyed as by a lamb.

And so he led him foaming and panting to the King—
But 'No !' said Don Alphonso, 'it were a shameful thing
That peerless Bavieca should ever be bestrid
By any mortal but Bivar—mount, mount again, my Cid !'

THE EXCOMMUNICATION OF THE CID.

[The last specimen I shall give of the Cid-ballads, is one the subject of which is evidently of the most apocryphal cast. It is, however, so far as I recollect, the only one of all that immense collection that is quoted or alluded to in Don Quixote. 'Sancho,' cried the knight, 'I am afraid of being excommunicated for having laid violent hands upon a man in holy orders. *Juxta illud; si quis suadente diabolo, &c.* But yet, now I think better on it, I never touched him with my hands, but only with my lance; be sides, I did not in the least suspect I had to do with priests, whom I honor and revere as every good Catholic and faithful Christian ought to do, but rather took them to be evil spirits. Well, let the worst come to the worst, I remember what befel the Cid Ruy Diaz, when he broke to pieces the chair of a king's ambassador in the Pope's presence, for which he was excommunicated; which did not hinder the worthy Rodrigo de Bivar from behaving himself that day like a valorous knight and a man of honor.']

It was when from Spain across the main the Cid had come to Rome.
He chanced to see chairs four and three beneath Saint Peter's dome :
'Now tell, I pray, what chairs be they ?'—'Seven kings do sit thereon,
As well doth suit, all at the foot of the holy Father's throne.

'The Pope he sitteth above them all, that they may kiss his toe,
Below the keys the Flower-de-lys doth make a gallant show ;
For his great puissance, the King of France next to the Pope may sit,
The rest more low, all in a row, as doth their station fit.'

'Ha !' quoth the Cid, 'now, God forbid ! it is a shame I wiss
To see the Castle planted below the Flower-de-lys.
No harm, I hope, good Father Pope, although I move thy chair.'
—In pieces small he kicked it all ('twas of the ivory fair) :—

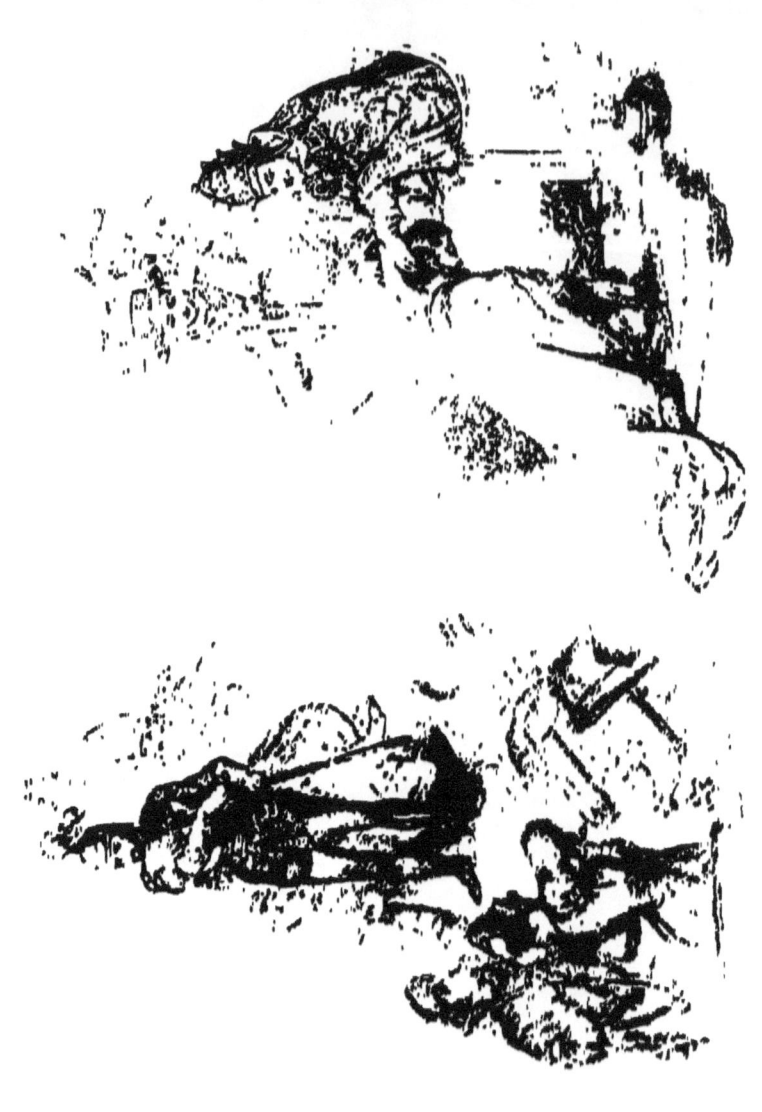

The Pope's own seat he from his feet did kick it far away,
And the Spanish chair he planted upon its place that day ;
Above them all he planted it, and laughed right bitterly :
Looks sour and bad I trow he had, as grim as grim might be.

Now when the Pope was aware of this, he was an angry man,
His lips that night, with solemn rite, pronounced the awful ban :
The curse of God, who died on rood, was on that sinner's head ;
To hell and wo man's soul must go if once that curse be said

I wot, when the Cid was aware of this, a woful man was he,
At dawn of day he came to pray at the blessed Father's knee :
Absolve me, blessed Father ! have pity on my prayer,
Absolve my soul, and penance I for my sin will bear.

' Who is this sinner,' quoth the Pope, ' that at my foot doth kneel ?'
' I am Rodrigo Diaz—a poor baron of Castile.'
Much marvelled all were in the hall, when that name they heard him say
' Rise up, rise up !' the Pope he said, ' I do thy guilt away ;—

' I do thy guilt away,' he said—' my curse I blot it out :
God save Rodrigo Diaz, my Christian champion stout ;
I trow, if I had known thee, my grief it had been sore,
To curse Ruy Diaz de Bivar, God's scourge upon the Moor.'

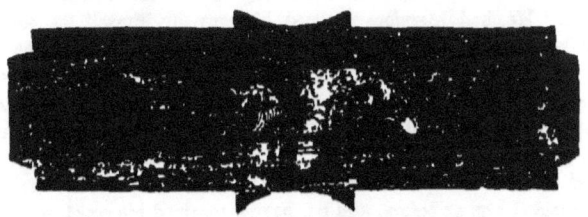

GARCI PEREZ DE VARGAS

[THE crowns of Castile and Leon being at length joined in the person of King Ferdinand, surnamed *El Santo*, the authority of the Moors in Spain was destined to receive many severe blows from the united efforts of two Christian states which had in former times too often exerted their vigour against each other. The most important event of King Ferdinand's reign was the conquest of Seville, which great city yielded to his arms in the year 1248, after sustaining a long and arduous siege of sixteen months.

Don Garci Perez de Vargas was one of the most distinguished warriors who on this occasion fought under the banners of Ferdinand; and accordingly there are many ballads of which he is the hero. The incident celebrated in that which follows, is thus told, with a few variations, in Mariana, (Book xiii., Chap. 7.)—

'Above all others there signalised himself in these affairs that Garci Perez de Vargas, a native of Toledo, of whose valour so many marvellous and almost incredible achievements are related. One day, about the beginning of the siege, this Garci and another with him were riding by the side of the river, at some distance from the outposts, when of a sudden there came upon them a party of seven Moors on horseback. The companion of Perez was for returning immediately, but he replied that 'Never, even though he should lose his life for it, would he consent to the baseness of flight.' With that his companion riding off, Perez armed himself, closed his visor, and put his lance in the rest. But the enemies, when they knew who it was, declined the combat. He had therefore pursued his way by himself for some space, when he perceived that in lacing the head-piece and shutting the visor he had, by inadvertence, dropped his scarf. He immediately returned upon his steps that he might seek for it. The King, as it happened, had his eyes upon Perez all this time, for the royal tent looked towards the place where he was riding; and he never doubted that the knight had turned back for the purpose of provoking the Moors to the combat. But they avoided him as before, and he, having regained his scarf, came in safety to the camp.

GARCI PEREZ DE VARGAS.

Page 47.

'The honor of the action was much increased by this circumstance, that, although frequently pressed to disclose the name of the gentleman who had deserted him in that moment of danger, Perez would never consent to do so, for his modesty was equal to his bravery.'

A little farther on Mariana relates that Garci Perez had a dispute with another gentleman, who thought proper to assert that Garci had no right to assume the coat of arms which he wore. 'A sally having been made by the Moors, that gentleman, among many more, made his escape, but Garci stood firm to his post, and never came back to the camp until the Moors were driven again into the city. He came with his shield all bruised and battered to the place where the gentleman was standing, and pointing to the effaced bearing which was on it, said, "Indeed, sir, it must be confessed that you show more respect than I do to this same coat-of-arms, for you keep yours bright and unsullied, while mine is sadly discoloured." The gentleman was sorely ashamed, and thenceforth Garci Perez bore his achievement without gainsaying or dispute.']

———————

KING FERDINAND alone did stand one day upon the hill,
Surveying all his leaguer, and the ramparts of Seville ;
The sight was grand, when Ferdinand by proud Seville was lying,
O'er tower and tree far off to see the Christian banners flying.

Down chanced the King his eye to fling, where far the camp below
Two gentlemen along the glen were riding soft and slow ;
As void of fear each cavalier seemed to be riding there,
As some strong hound may pace around the roebuck's thicket lair.

It was Don Garci Perez, and he would breathe the air,
And he had ta'en a knight with him, that as lief had been elsewhere ;
For soon this knight to Garci said, ' Ride, ride we, or we're lost !
I see the glance of helm and lance—it is the Moorish host ! '

The Lord of Vargas turned him round, his trusty squire was near—
The helmet on his brow he bound, his gauntlet grasped the spear ;
With that upon his saddle-tree he planted him right steady—
' Now come,' quoth he, ' whoe'er they be, I trow they'll find us ready.'

By this the knight who rode with him had turned his horse's head,
And up the glen in fearful trim unto the camp had fled.
'Ha! gone?' quoth Garci Perez :—he smiled, and said no more,
But slowly, with his esquire, rode as he rode before.

It was the Count Lorenzo, just then it happened so,
He took his stand by Ferdinand, and with him gazed below;
'My liege,' quoth he, 'seven Moors I see a-coming from the wood,
Now bring they all the blows they may, I trow they'll find us good;
But it is Don Garci Perez—if his cognizance they know,
I guess it will be little pain to give them blow for blow.'

The Moors from forth the greenwood came riding one by one,
A gallant troop with armour resplendent in the sun;
Full haughty was their bearing, as o'er the sward they came,
While the calm Lord of Vargas his march was still the same.

They stood drawn up in order, while past them all rode he,
For when upon his shield they saw the sable blazonry,
And the wings of the Black Eagle, that o'er his crest were spread,
They knew Don Garci Perez, and never word they said.

He took the casque from off his head, and gave it to the squire,
'My friend,' quoth he, 'no need I see why I my brows should tire.
But as he doffed the helmet, he saw his scarf was gone—
'I've dropped it sure,' quoth Garci, 'when I put my helmet on.

He looked around and saw the scarf, for still the Moors were near,
And they had picked it from the sward, and looped it on a spear;
'These Moors,' quoth Garci Perez, 'uncourteous Moors they be—
Now, by my soul, the scarf they stole, yet durst not question me!

Now, reach once more my helmet.'—The esquire said him nay,
'For a silken string why should ye fling perchance your life away?'
—'I had it from my lady,' quoth Garci, 'long ago,
And never Moor that scarf, be sure, in proud Seville shall show.'--

But when the Moslem saw him they stood in firm array,
—He rode among their armed throng, he rode right furiously;
—'Stand, stand, ye thieves and robbers, lay down my lady's pledge!'
He cried:—and ever as he cried they felt his faulchion's edge.

That day the Lord of Vargas came to the camp alone;
The scarf, his lady's largess, around his breast was thrown;
Bare was his head, his sword was red, and from his pommel strung.
Seven turbans green, sore hacked I ween, before Don Garci hung.

THE POUNDER.

[A BALLAD concerning another doughty knight of the same family, and most
probably, considering the date, a brother of Garci Perez de Vargas. Its story
is thus alluded to by Don Quixote, in the chapter of the Windmills :—
  'However, the loss of his lance was no small affliction to him ; and as he
was making his complaint about it to his squire—I have read, said he,
friend Sancho, that a certain Spanish knight, whose name was Diego Perez
de Vargas, having broken his sword in the heat of an engagement, pulled up
by the roots a wild olive tree, or at least, tore down a massy branch, and
did such wonderful execution, crushing and grinding so many Moors with
it that day, that he won for himself and his posterity the surname of The
Pounder, or Bruiser. [*Machuca*, from *Machucar*, to pound as in a mortar.] I
tell this, because I intend to tear up the next oak, or holm-tree, we meet ;
with the trunk whereof I hope to perform such deeds that thou wilt
esteem thyself happy in having had the honour to behold them, and been
the ocular witness of achievements which posterity will scarce be able to
believe.—Heaven grant you may! cried Sancho : I believe it all, because
your worship says it.']

THE Christians have beleaguered the famous walls of Xeres :
Among them are Don Alvar and Don Diego Perez,
And many other gentlemen who, day succeeding day,
Give challenge to the Saracen and all his chivalry.

When rages the hot battle before the gates of Xeres,
By trace of gore ye may explore the dauntless path of Perez :
No knight like Don Diego—no sword like his is found
In all the host, to hew the boast of Paynims to the ground.

It fell one day when furiously they battled on he plain,
Diego shivered both his lance and trusty blade in twain ;
The Moors that saw it shouted, for esquire none was near
To serve Diego at his need with falchion, mace, or spear.

Loud, loud he blew his bugle, sore troubled was his eye,
But by God's grace before his face there stood a tree full nigh—
An olive-tree with branches strong, close by the wall of Xeres:
'Yon goodly bough will serve, I trow,' quoth Don Diego Perez.

A gnarled branch he soon did wrench down from that olive strong,
Which o'er his head-piece brandishing, he spurs among the throng.
God wot! full many a Pagan must in his saddle reel:
What leech may cure, what beadsman shrive, if once that weight ye feel!

But when Don Alvar saw him thus bruising down the foe,
Quoth he, 'I've seen some flail-armed man belabor barley so:
Sure mortal mould did ne'er enfold such mastery of power—
Let's call Diego Perez THE POUNDER, from this hour.'

THE MURDER OF THE MASTER.

[THE next four ballads relate to the history of DON PEDRO, King of Castile, called THE CRUEL.

An ingenious person not long ago published a work, the avowed purpose of which was to prove that Tiberius was a humane and contemplative prince, who retired to the island of Capreæ only that he might the better indulge in the harmless luxury of philosophic meditation :—and, in like manner, Pedro the Cruel has found, in these latter times, his defenders and apologists ; above all, Voltaire.

There may be traced, without doubt, in the circumstances which attended his accession, something to palliate the atrocity of several of his bloody acts. His father had treated his mother with contempt : he had not only entertained, as his mistress, in her lifetime, a lady of the powerful family of Guzman, but actually proclaimed that lady his queen, and brought up her sons as princes in his palace ; nay, he had even betrayed some

intentions of violating, in their favor, the order of succession, and the rights
of Pedro. And, accordingly, no sooner was Alphonso dead, and Pedro
acknowledged by the nobility, than Leonora de Guzman, and her sons,
whether from consciousness of guilt, or from fear of violence, or from both
of these causes, betook themselves to various places of strength, where
they endeavoured to defend themselves against the authority of the new
king. After a little time, matters were accommodated by the interference
of friends, and Donna Leonora took up her residence at Seville; but
Pedro was suddenly, while in that city, seized with a distemper which his
physicians said must, in all probability, have a mortal termination; and
during his confinement (which lasted for several weeks) many intrigues
were set a-foot, and the pretensions of various candidates for the throne
openly canvassed among the nobility of Castile. Whether the king had,
on his recovery, discovered anything indicative of treasonous intentions in
the recent conduct of Leonora and her family—(which, all things considered, seems not improbable)—or whether he merely suffered himself (as
was said at the time) to be over-persuaded by the vindictive arguments
of his own mother, the queen-dowager, the fact is certain, that in the
course of a few days Donna Leonora was arrested, and put to death,
by Pedro's command, in the castle of Talaveyra. Don Fadrique, or
Frederick, one of her sons, who had obtained the dignity of Master of
the Order of St. Iago, fled upon this into Portugal, and fortified himself in
the city of Coimbra; while another of them, Don Enrique, or Henry,
Lord of Trastamara, took refuge at the Court of Arragon, openly
renouncing his allegiance to the crown of Castile, and professing himself
henceforth, in all things, the subject and vassal of the prince who gave
him protection.

Henry of Trastamara was, from this time, the declared and active
enemy of his brother; and in consequence of his influence, and that of his
mother's kindred, but most of all in consequence of Don Pedro's own
atrocious proceedings, Castile itself was filled with continual tumults and
insurrections.

Don Fadrique, however, made his peace with Pedro. After a lapse of many
months, he was invited to come to the court at Seville and take his share
in the amusements of an approaching tournament. He accepted the
invitation, but was received with terrible coldness, and immediately
executed within the palace. The friends of Pedro asserted that the king
had that very day detected Don Fadrique in a correspondence with his
brother Henry and the Arragonese; while popular belief attributed the

slaughter of the Master to the unhappy influence which the too-celebrated Maria de Padilla had long ere this begun to exercise over Pedro's mind.

Maria was often, in consequence of her close intimacy with Jews, called by the name of their hated race; but she was in reality not only of Christian, but of noble descent in Spain. However that might be, Pedro found her in the family of his minister, Albuquerque, where she had been brought up, loved her with all the violence of his temper, and made her his wife in all things but the name. Although political motives induced him, not long afterwards, to contract an alliance with a princess of the French blood royal—the unfortunate Blanche of Bourbon—he lived with the young queen but a few days, and then deserted her for ever, for the sake of this beautiful, jealous, and imperious mistress, whom he declared to be his true wife.

The reader will observe that there is a strange peculiarity in the structure of the ballad which narrates the Murder of the Master of St. Iago. The unfortunate Fadrique is introduced at the beginning of it as telling his own story, and so he carries it on, in the first person, until the order for his execution is pronounced by Pedro. The sequel is given as if by another voice. I can suppose this singularity to have had a musical origin.

The Master was slain in the year 1358.]

I sat alone in Coimbra—the town myself had ta'en,
When came into my chamber a messenger from Spain;
There was no treason in his look, an honest look he wore;
I from his hand the letter took—my brother's seal it bore.

'Come, brother dear, the day draws near'—('twas thus bespoke the King)—
'For plenar court and knightly sport within the listed ring.'—
Alas! unhappy Master, I easy credence lent;
Alas! for fast and faster I at his bidding went.

When I set off from Coimbra, and passed the bound of Spain,
I had a goodly company of spearmen in my train—
A gallant force, a score of horse, and sturdy mules thirteen:
With joyful heart I held my course—my years were young and green.

A journey of good fifteen days within the week was done—
I halted not, though signs I got, dark tokens many a one;
A strong stream mastered horse and mule—I lost my poniard fine—
And left a page within the pool—a faithful page of mine;

Yet on to proud Seville I rode; when to the gate I came,
Before me stood a man of God, to warn me from the same;
The words he spake I would not hear, his grief I would not see,
I seek, said I, my brother dear—I will not stop for thee.

No lists were closed upon the sand, for royal tourney dight;
No pawing horse was seen to stand—I saw no armed knight—
Yet aye I gave my mule the spur, and hastened through the town:
I stopped before his palace-door—then gaily leapt I down.

They shut the door—my trusty score of friends were left behind;
I would not hear their whispered fear—no harm was in my mind;
I greeted Pedro, but he turned—I wot his look was cold;
His brother from his knee he spurned;—'Stand off, thou Master bold!'—

'Stand off, stand off, thou traitor strong!'—'twas thus he said to me—
'Thy time on earth shall not be long—what brings thee to my knee?
My lady craves a new-year's gift, and I will keep my word;
Thy head methinks may serve the shift—Good yeoman, draw thy sword!'

The Master lay upon the floor ere well that word was said:
Then in a charger off they bore his pale and bloody head;
They brought it to Padilla's chair—they bowed them on the knee;
'King Pedro greets thee, lady fair, his gift he sends to thee.'—

She gazed upon the Master's head, her scorn it could not scare,
And cruel were the words she said, and proud her glances were;
' Thou now shalt pay, thou traitor base! the debt of many a year;
My dog shall lick that haughty face;—no more that lip shall sneer.'

She seized it by the clotted hair, and o'er the window flung;
The mastiff smelt it in his lair—forth at her cry he sprung;
The mastiff that had crouched so low to lick the Master's hand,
He tossed the morsel to and fro, and licked it on the sand.

And ever as the mastiff tore his bloody teeth were shown,
With growl and snort he made his sport, and picked it to the bone;
The baying of the beast was loud, and swiftly on the street
There gathered round a gaping crowd to see the mastiff eat.

Then out and spake King Pedro—' What governance is this?
The rabble rout, my gate without, torment my dogs, I wiss.'
Then out and spake King Pedro's page—' It is the Master's head;
The mastiff tears it in his rage—therewith they him have fed.'

Then out and spake the ancient nurse, that nursed the brothers twain—
' On thee, King Pedro, lies the curse—thy brother thou hast slain;
A thousand harlots there may be within the realm of Spain,
But where is she can give to thee thy brother back again?'

Came darkness o'er King Pedro's brow, when thus he heard her say;
He sorely rued the accursed vow he had fulfilled that day;
He passed unto his paramour, where on her couch she lay,
Leaning from out her painted bower to see the mastiff's play.

He drew her to a dungeon dark, a dungeon strong and deep;
' My father's son lies stiff and stark, and there are few to weep.
Fadriqué's blood for vengeance calls—his cry is in mine ear—
Thou art the cause, thou harlot false!—in darkness lie thou here.'

THE DEATH OF QUEEN BLANCHE.

——◆——

[THAT Pedro was accessory to the violent death of this young and innocent princess whom he had married, and immediately afterwards deserted
for ever, there can be no doubt.　This deed was avenged abundantly;
for it certainly led, in the issue, to the downfal and death of Pedro.
Mariana says, very briefly, that the injuries sustained by Queen Blanche
had so much offended many of Pedro's own nobility, that they drew up
a formal remonstrance, and presented it to him in a style sufficiently
formidable; and that he, his proud and fierce temper being stung to
madness by what he considered an unjustifiable interference with his
domestic concerns, immediately gave orders for the poisoning of Blanche
in her prison.　In the old French Memoirs of Du Guesclin a much more improbable story is told at great length.　The Queen Blanche, according to this account,
had been banished to the Castle of Medina Sidonia—the adjoining territory
being assigned to her for her maintenance.　One of her vassals, a Jew,
presumed to do his homage in the usual fashion, that is, by kissing Blanche
on the cheek, ere his true character was suspected either by her or her
attendants.　No sooner was the man known to be a Jew, than he was driven
from the presence of the queen with every mark of insult; and this sunk so
deeply into his mind that he determined to revenge himself, if possible, by
the death of Blanche.　He told his story to Maria de Padilla, who prevailed
on the king to suffer him to take his own measures; and he accordingly
surprised the castle by night, at the head of a troop of his own countrymen,
and butchered the unhappy lady.　The ballad itself is, in all likelihood, as
trust-worthy as any other authority; the true particulars of such a crime were
pretty sure to be kept concealed.]

'MARIA DE PADILLA, be not thus of dismal mood,
For if I twice have wedded me, it all was for thy good;
But if upon Queen Blanche ye will that I some scorn should show,
For a banner to Medina my messenger shall go—
The work shall be of Blanche's tears, of Blanche's blood the ground;
Such pennon shall they weave for thee, such sacrifice be found.'

Then to the Lord of Ortis, that excellent baron,
He said, 'Now hear me, Ynigo, forthwith for this begone.'
Then answer made Don Ynigo, 'Such gift I ne'er will bring,
For he that harmeth Lady Blanche doth harm my lord the king.'

Then Pedro to his chamber went—his cheek was burning red—
And to a bowman of his guard the dark command he said.
The bowman to Medina passed; when the queen beheld him near,
'Alas!' she said, 'my maidens, he brings my death, I fear.'

Then said the archer, bending low—'The King's commandment take,
And see thy soul be ordered well with God that did it make:
For lo! thine hour is come, therefrom no refuge may there be.'—
Then gently spake the Lady Blanche 'My friend, I pardon thee;
Do what thou wilt, so be the King hath his commandment given:
Deny me not confession—if so, forgive ye, Heaven!'

Much grieved the bowman for her tears, and for her beauty's sake,
While thus Queen Blanche of Bourbon her last complaint did make;—
'O France! my noble country—O blood of high Bourbon!
Not eighteen years have I seen out before my life is gone.
The King hath never known me.   A virgin true I die.
Whate'er I've done, to proud Castile no treason e'er did I.

'The crown they put upon my head was a crown of blood and sighs,
God grant me soon another crown more precious in the skies!'—
These words she spake, then down she knelt, and took the bowman's blow;
Her tender neck was cut in twain, and out her blood did flow.

THE DEATH OF DON PEDRO.

[THE reader may remember that when Don Pedro had, by his excessive
cruelties, quite alienated from himself the hearts of the great majority of
his people, Don Henry of Trastamara, his natural brother, who had spent
many years in exile, returned suddenly into Spain with a formidable
band of French auxiliaries, by whose aid he drove Pedro out of his kingdom.
The voice of the nation was on Henry's side, and he took possession of the
throne without further opposition. Pedro, after his treatment of Queen
Blanche, could have nothing to hope from the crown of France, so he
immediately threw himself into the arms of England. And Edward the
Black Prince, who then commanded in Gascony, had more than one
obvious reason for taking up his cause.

The Prince of Wales marched with Don Pedro into Spain, at the head of
an army of English and Gascon veterans, whose disciplined valor, Mariana
very frankly confesses, gave them a decided superiority over the Spanish
soldiery of the time. Henry was so unwise as to set his stake upon a
battle, and was totally defeated in the field of Najara. Unable to rally
his flying troops, he was compelled to make his escape beyond the Pyrenees;
and Don Pedro once more established himself in his kingdom. The battle
of Najara took place in 1366. But, in 1368, when the Black Prince
had retired again into Gascony, Henry, in his turn, came back from
exile with a small but gallant army, most of whom were French,
commanded by the celebrated Bertram Du Glessquin—or, as he is
more commonly called, Du Guesclin—and animated, as was natural, by
strong thirst of vengeance for the insults, which, in the person of
Blanche, Pedro had heaped upon the royal line of their country and
the blood of Saint Louis.—Henry advanced into the heart of La Mancha,

and there encountered Don Pedro, at the head of an army six times more numerous than that which he commanded, but composed in a great measure of Jews, Saracens, and Portuguese—miscellaneous auxiliaries, who gave way before the ardour of the French chivalry—so that Henry remained victorious, and Pedro was forced to take refuge in the neighboring castle of Montiel. That fortress was so strictly blockaded by the successful enemy, that the king was compelled to attempt his escape by night, with only twelve in his retinue—Ferdinand de Castro being the person of most note among them. As they wandered in the dark, they were encountered by a body of French cavalry making the rounds, commanded by an adventurous knight, called Le Bègue de Villaines. Compelled to surrender, Don Pedro put himself under the safeguard of this officer, promising him a rich ransom if he would conceal him from the knowledge of his brother Henry. The knight, according to Froissart, promised him concealment, and conveyed him to his own quarters. But in the course of an hour, Henry was apprised that he was taken, and came with some of his followers, to the tent of Allan de la Houssaye, where his unfortunate brother had been placed. On entering it he exclaimed, 'Where is that whoreson and Jew who calls himself King of Castile?'—Pedro, as proud and fearless as he was cruel, stepped instantly forward and replied, 'Here I stand, the lawful son and heir of Don Alphonso, and it is thou that art but a false bastard.' The rival brethren instantly grappled like lions, the French knights and Du Guesclin himself looking on. Henry drew his poniard, and wounded Pedro in the face, but his body was defended by a coat of mail;—a violent struggle ensued :—Henry fell across a bench, and his brother, being uppermost, had well-nigh mastered him, when one of Henry's followers, seizing Don Pedro by the leg, turned him over, and his master, thus at length gaining the upper hand, instantly stabbed the king to the heart.—Froissart calls this man the Vicomte de Roquebetyn, and others the Bastard of Anisse. Menard, in his history of Du Guesclin, says, that while all around gazed like statues on the furious struggle of the brothers, Du Guesclin exclaimed to this attendant of Henry; 'What! will you stand by and see your master placed at such a pass by a false renegade?—Make forward and aid him, for well you may.'

Pedro's head was cut off, and his remains were meanly buried. They were afterwards disinterred by his daughter, the wife of our own John of Gaunt, 'time-honoured Lancaster,' and deposited in Seville, with the honors due to his rank. His memory was regarded with a strange

mixture of horror and compassion, which recommended him as a subject for
legend and for romance. He had caused his innocent wife to be assassinated
—had murdered three of his brothers—and committed numberless cruelties
upon his subjects. He had, which the age deemed equally scandalous, held
a close intimacy with the Jews and Saracens, and had enriched himself at
the expense of the Church. Yet, in spite of all these crimes, his undaunted
bravery and energy of character, together with the strange circumstances of
his death, excited milder feelings towards his memory.

The following ballad, which describes the death of Don Pedro, was
translated by a friend (Sir Walter Scott.) It is quoted more than once by
Cervantes in Don Quixote.]

HENRY and King Pedro clasping,
   Hold in straining arms each other ;
Tugging hard and closely grasping,
   Brother proves his strength with brother.

Harmless pastime, sport fraternal,
   Blends not thus their limbs in strife ;
Either aims, with rage infernal,
   Naked dagger, sharpened knife.

Close Don Henry grapples Pedro,
   Pedro holds Don Henry strait,
Breathing, this, triumphant fury,
   That, despair and mortal hate.

Sole spectator of the struggle,
   Stands Don Henry's page afar,
In the chase who bore his bugle,
   And who bore his sword in war.

THE DEATH OF DON QUIXOTE

Down they go in deadly wrestle,
  Down upon the earth they go,
Fierce King Pedro has the vantage,
  Stout Don Henry falls below.

Marking then the fatal crisis,
  Up the page of Henry ran,
By the waist he caught Don Pedro,
  Aiding thus the fallen man :—

  King to place, or to depose him,
    Dwelleth not in my desire,
  But the duty which he owes him
    To his master pays the squire.'—

Now Don Henry has the upmost,
  Now King Pedro lies beneath :
In his heart his brother's poniard
  Instant finds its bloody sheath.

Thus with mortal gasp and quiver,
  While the blood in bubbles welled,
Fled the fiercest soul that ever
  In a Christian bosom dwelled.

THE PROCLAMATION OF KING HENRY.

[THE following ballad, taking up the story where it is left in the preceding one, gives us the proclamation and coronation of Don Henry, surnamed, from the courtesy of his manners, *El Cavallero*, and the grief of Pedro's lovely and unhappy mistress, Maria de Padilla. From its structure and versification, I have no doubt it is of much more modern origin than most of those in the first Cancionero.

The picture which Mariana gives us of Don Pedro, the hero of so many atrocious and tragical stories, is very striking. 'He was pale of complexion,' says the historian (book xvi. chap. 10) 'his features were high and well formed, and stamped with a certain authority of majesty, his hair red, his figure erect, even to stiffness; he was bold and determined in action and in council; his bodily frame sank under no fatigues, his spirit under no weight of difficulty or of danger. He was passionately fond of hawking and all violent exercises. In the beginning of his reign, he administered justice among private individuals with perfect integrity. But even then were visible in him the rudiments of those vices which grew with his age, and finally led him to his ruin; such as a general contempt and scorn of mankind, an insulting tongue, a proud and difficult ear, even to those of his household. These faults were discernible even in his tender years; to them, as he advanced in life, were added avarice, dissolution in luxury, an utter hardness of heart, and a remorseless cruelty.']

At the feet of Don Henrique now King Pedro dead is lying,
Not that Henry's might was greater, but that blood to Heaven was crying;
Though deep the dagger had its sheath within his brother's breast,
Firm on the frozen throat beneath Don Henry's foot is pressed.

MARIA DE PADILLA.

Page 63.

So dark and sullen is the glare of Pedro's lifeless eyes,
Still half he fears what slumbers there to vengeance may arise.
So stands the brother—on his brow the mark of blood is seen,
Yet had he not been Pedro's Cain, his Cain had Pedro been.

Close round the scene of cursed strife, the armed knights appear
Of either band, with silent thoughts of joyfulness or fear;
All for a space in silence the fratricide survey—
Then sudden bursts the mingling voice of triumph and dismay.

Glad shout on shout from Henry's host ascends unto the sky;
'God save King Henry—save the King—King Henry!' is their cry.
But Pedro's barons clasp their brows—in sadness stand they near—
Whate'er to others he had been, their friend lies murdered here.

The deed, say those, was justly done—a tyrant's soul is sped;
These ban and curse the traitorous blow by which a King is dead.
'Now see,' cries one, 'how Heaven's amand asserts the people's rights!
Another—'God will judge the hand that God's anointed smites!'

'The Lord's vicegerent,' quoth a priest, 'is sovereign of the land,
And he rebels 'gainst Heaven's behest, that slights his King's command!'
'Now Heaven be witness, if he sinned,' thus speaks a gallant young,
'The fault was in Padilla's eye, that o'er him magic flung;—

'Or if no magic be her blame, so heavenly fair is she,
The wisest, for so bright a dame, might well a sinner be!
Let none speak ill of Pedro—no Roderick hath he been—
He dearly loved fair Spain although 'tis true he slew the Queen.'

The words he spake they all might hear, yet none vouchsafe reply—
'God save great Henry—save the King—King Henry!' is the cry;
While Pedro's liegemen turn aside, their groans are in your ear—
'Whate'er to others he hath been, our friend lies slaughtered here!'

Nor paltry souls are wanting among King Pedro's band,
That, now their king is dead, draw near to kiss his murderer's hand :
The false cheek clothes it in a smile, and laughs the hollow eye,
And wags the traitor tongue the while with flattery's ready lie.

The valor of the King that *is*—the justice of his cause—
The blindness and the tyrannies of him, the King that *was*—
All—all are doubled in their speech, yet truth enough is there
To sink the spirit shivering near, in darkness of despair.

The murder of the Master, the tender Infants' doom,
And blessed Blanche's thread of life snapped short in dungeon's gloom,
With tragedies yet unrevealed, that stained the King's abode,
By lips his bounty should have sealed are blazoned black abroad.

Whom served he most at others' cost, most loud they rend the sky—
' God save great Henry—save our King—King Henry !' is the cry :
But still, amid too many foes, the grief is in your ear
Of dead King Pedro's faithful few—' Alas ! our lord lies here !'

But others' tears, and others' groans, what are they matched with thine,
Maria de Padilla—thou fatal concubine !
Because she is King Henry's slave, the lady weepeth sore,
Because she's Pedro's widowed love, alas ! she weepeth more.

' O Pedro ! Pedro !' hear her cry—' how often did I say
That wicked counsel and weak trust would haste thy life away !'—
She stands upon her turret-top, she looks down from on high,
Where mantled in his bloody cloak she sees her lover lie.

Low lies King Pedro in his blood, while bending down ye see
Caitiffs that trembled ere he spake, crouched at his murderer's knees ;
They place the sceptre in his hand, and on his head the crown,
And trumpets clear are blown, and bells are merry through the town.

The sun shines bright, and the gay rout with clamours rend the sky,
'God save great Henry—save the King—King Henry!' is the cry;
But the pale lady weeps above, with many a bitter tear:
Whate'er he was, he was her love, and he lies slaughtered here!

At first, in silence down her cheek the drops of sadness roll,
But rage and anger come to break the sorrow of her soul;
The triumph of her haters—the gladness of their cries,
Enkindle flames of ire and scorn within her tearful eyes.

In her hot cheek the blood mounts high, as she stands gazing down,
Now on proud Henry's royal state, his robe and golden crown—
And now upon the trampled cloak that hides not from her view
The slaughtered Pedro's marble brow and lips of livid hue.

With furious grief she twists her hands among her long black hairs,
And all from off her lovely brow the blameless locks she tears;
She tears the ringlets from her front, and scatters all the pearls
King Pedro's hand had planted among the raven curls:

'Stop, caitiff tongues!'—they hear her not—'King Pedro's love am I!—
They heed her not—'God save the King—great Henry!' still they cry.
She rends her hair, she wrings her hands, but none to help is near—
'God look in vengeance on their deed, my lord lies murdered here!'

Away she flings her garments, her broidered veil and vest,
As if they should behold her love within her lovely breast,
As if to call upon her foes the constant heart to see,
Where Pedro's form is still enshrined, and evermore shall be.

But none on fair Maria looks, by none her breast is seen—
Save angry Heaven remembering well the murder of the Queen,
The wounds of jealous harlot rage, which virgin blood must stanch,
And all the scorn that mingled in the bitter cup of Blanche.

F

The utter coldness of neglect that haughty spirit stings,
As if a thousand fiends were there, with all their flapping wings;
She wraps the veil about her head, as if 'twere all a dream—
The love—the murder—and the wrath—and that rebellious scream.

For still there's shouting on the plain, and spurring far and nigh—
'God save the King—Amen! amen!—King Henry!' is the cry;
While Pedro all alone is left upon his bloody bier—
Not one remains to cry to God, 'Our lord lies murdered here!'

THE LORD OF BUTRAGO.

[THE incident to which the following ballad relates, is supposed to have occurred on the famous field of Aljubarrota, where King Juan the First of Castile was defeated by the Portuguese. The king, who was at the time in a feeble state of health, exposed himself very much during the action; and being wounded, had great difficulty in making his escape. The battle was fought A. D. 1385.]

'YOUR horse is faint, my King—my Lord! your gallant horse is sick—
His limbs are torn, his breast is gored, on his eye the film is thick;
Mount, mount on mine, oh, mount apace, I pray thee, mount and fly!
Or in my arms I'll lift your grace—their trampling hoofs are nigh!

'My King—my King! you're wounded sore—the blood runs from your feet;
But only lay a hand before, and I'll lift you to your seat:
Mount, Juan, for they gather fast!—I hear their coming cry—
Mount, mount, and ride for jeopardy—I'll save you though I die!

'Stand, noble steed! this hour of need—be gentle as a lamb:
I'll kiss the foam from off thy mouth—thy master dear I am—
Mount, Juan, mount! whate'er betide, away the bridle fling,
And plunge the rowels in his side.—My horse shall save my King!

'Nay, never speak; my sires, Lord King, received their land from yours,
And joyfully their blood shall spring, so be it thine secures:
If I should fly, and thou, my King, be found among the dead,
How could I stand 'mong gentlemen, such scorn on my grey head?

'Castile's proud dames shall never point the finger of disdain,
And say there's one that ran away when our good lords were slain!—
I leave Diego in your care—you'll fill his father's place:
Strike, strike the spur, and never spare—God's blessing on your grace!'

So spake the brave Montañez, Butrago's lord was he;
And turned him to the coming host in steadfastness and glee;
He flung himself among them, as they came down the hill—
He died, God wot! but not before his sword had drunk its fill.

THE KING OF ARRAGON.

[THE following little ballad represents the supposed feelings of Ferdinand,
King of Arragon, on surveying Naples, after he had at last obtained possession of that city, and driven René of Anjou from the south of Italy. 'The
King of Arragon,' says Mariana, 'entered Naples as victor, on the morning
of Sunday, the second of June, in the year of our Lord one thousand, four
hundred, and forty two.'—The brother, whose death is represented as sad-
dening the King's triumph, was Don Pedro of Arragon, who was killed 'by
the fourth rebound of a cannon-ball,' very soon after the commencement of

the siege of Naples. 'When the King heard of these woful tidings,' says
Mariana, 'he hastened to the place where the body had been laid, and
kissing the breast of the dead man, said, "Alas, my brother, what different
things had I expected of thee! God help thy soul!" And with that he
wept and groaned, and then turning to his attendants, "Alas!" said he,
"my comrades, we have lost this day the flower of all our chivalry!"—Don
Pedro died in the bloom of his youth, being just twenty-seven years old, and
having never been married. He had been in many wars, and in all of them
he had won honour.'—(Mariana, Book xxi., Chap. 13.)—Who was the
favourite boy (Pagezico,) whose death the King also laments in the ballad, I
have not been able to find.]

One day the King of Arragon, from the old citadel,
Looked down upon the sea of Spain, as the billows rose and fell;
He looked on ship and galley, some coming and some going,
With all their prize of merchandise, and all their streamers flowing—

Some to Castile were sailing, and some to Barbary :—
And then he looked on Naples, that great city of the sea :
'O city!' saith the King, 'how great hath been thy cost,
For thee, I twenty years—my fairest years—have lost!

'By thee, I have lost a brother—never Hector was more brave—
High cavaliers have dropped their tears upon my brother's grave.
Much treasure hast thou cost me, and a little boy beside—
(Alas! thou woful city!)—for whom I would have died.'

THE VOW OF REQUAN

Page 69.

THE VOW OF REDUAN.

— ◆ —

[THE marriage of Ferdinand the Catholic and Donna Isabella having united the forces of Arragon and Castile, the total ruin of the Moorish power in Spain could no longer be deferred. The last considerable fragment of their once mighty possessions in the Peninsula was Granada; but the fate of Malaga gave warning of its inevitable fall, while internal dissensions, and the weakness of the reigning prince, hastened and facilitated that great object of Ferdinand's ambition.

The following is a version of certain parts of two ballads; indeed, the Moor Reduan is the hero of a great many more. The subject is, as the reader will perceive, the rash vow and tragical end of a young and gallant soldier, allied, as it would appear, to the blood of the last Moorish King of Granada, Boabdil,—or, as he is more generally called by the Spanish writers, *El Rey Chiquito*,—i. e.—the Little King.]

THUS said, before his lords, the King to Reduan :
'"Tis easy to get words—deeds get we as we can :
Rememberest thou the feast at which I heard thee saying,
'Twere easy in one night to make me Lord of Jaen !

' Well in my mind I hold the valiant vow was said ;
Fulfil it, boy ! and gold shall shower upon thy head ;
But bid a long farewell, if now thou shrink from doing,
To bower and bonnibell, thy feasting and thy wooing !

' I have forgot the oath, if such I e'er did plight—
But needs there plighted troth to make a soldier fight !
A thousand sabres bring—we'll see how we may thrive.'—
'One thousand !' quoth the King; 'I trow thou shalt have five !'

They passed the Elvira-gate, with banners all displayed,
They passed in mickle state, a noble cavalcade;
What proud and pawing horses, what comely cavaliers,
What bravery of targets, what glittering of spears!

What caftans blue and scarlet—what turbans pleached of green;
What waving of their crescents and plumages between;
What buskins and what stirrups—what rowels chased in gold!
What handsome gentlemen—what buoyant hearts and bold!

In midst, above them all, rides he who rules the band—
Yon feather white and tall is the token of command:
He looks to the Alhambra, whence bends his mother down—
'Now Alla save my boy, and merciful Mahoun!'—

But 'twas another sight—when Reduan drew near
To look upon the height where Jaen's towers appear;
The fosse was wide and deep, the walls both tall and strong,
And keep was matched with keep the battlements along.

It was a heavy sight—but most for Reduan:
He sighed, as well he might, ere thus his speech began:
'O Jaen! had I known how high thy bulwarks stand,
My tongue had not outgone the prowess of my hand.

'But since, in hasty cheer, I did my promise plight,
(What well might cost a year) to win thee in a night,
The pledge demands the paying. I would my soldiers brave
Were half as sure of Jaen as I am of my grave!

'My penitence comes late—my death lags not behind:
I yield me up to fate, since hope I may not find!'—
With that he turned him round;—'Now blow your trumpets high!'—
But every spearman frowned, and dark was every eye.

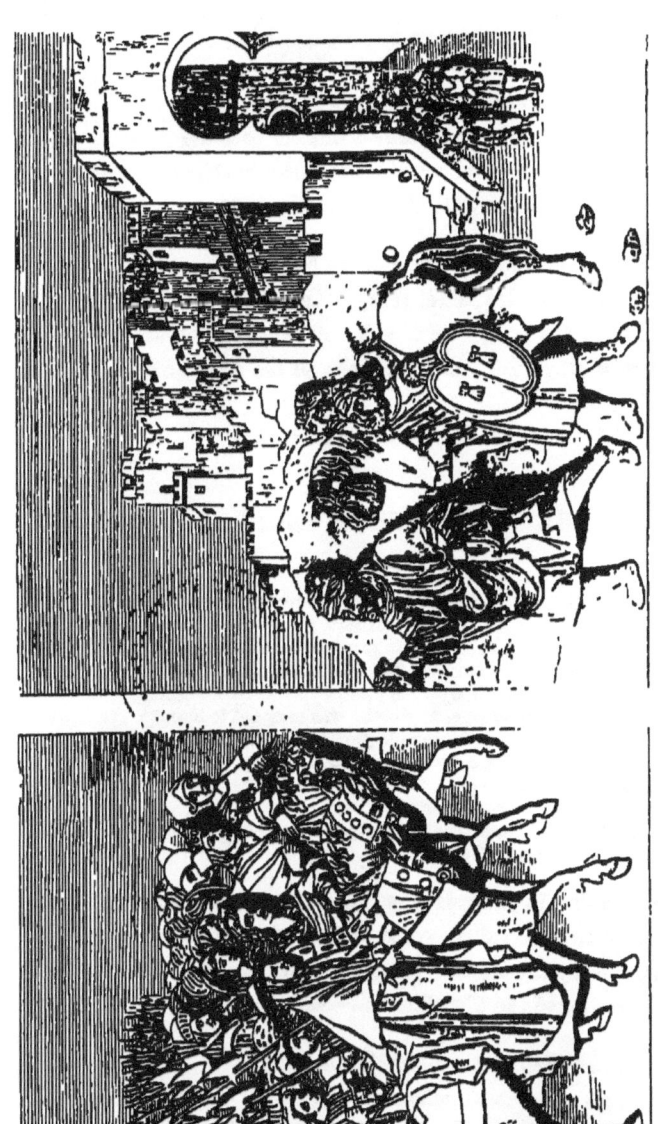

THE FLIGHT FROM GRANADA.

But when he was aware that they would fain retreat,
He spurred his bright bay mare—I wot her pace was fleet;
He rides beneath the walls, and shakes aloof his lance,
And to the Christians calls, if any will advance!

With that an arrow flew from o'er the battlement—
Young Reduan it slew, sheer through the breast it went;
He fell upon the green—'Farewell, my gallant bay!'—
Right soon, when this was seen, broke all the Moor array.

THE FLIGHT FROM GRANADA.

[THE following ballad describes the final departure of the weak and unfortunate
Boabdil from Granada. In point of fact, the Moorish King came out and
received Ferdinand and Isabella in great form and pomp, at the gates of his
lost city, presenting them with the keys on a cushion, and in abject terms
entreating their protection for his person.

The valley of Purchena, in Murcia, was assigned to him for his place of
residence, and a handsome revenue provided for the maintenance of him and
his family; but, after a little while, 'not having resolution' (as Mariana
expresses it) 'to endure a private life in the country where he had so long
reigned a King,' he went over to Barbary.

The entrance of Ferdinand and Isabella into Granada took place on Friday,
the 6th of January, 1492.]

THERE was crying in Granada when the sun was going down;
Some calling on the Trinity—some calling on Mahoun.
Here passed away the Koran—there in the Cross was borne—
And here was heard the Christian bell—and there the Moorish horn;

Te Deum Laudamus! was up the Alcala sung:
Down from the Alhambra's minarets were all the crescents flung;
The arms thereon of Arragon they with Castile's display;
One King comes in in triumph—one weeping goes away.

Thus cried the weeper, while his hands his old white beard did tear,
'Farewell, farewell, Granada! thou city without peer!
Woe, woe, thou pride of Heathendom! seven hundred years and more
Have gone since first the faithful thy royal sceptre bore!

'Thou wert the happy mother of an high renowned race;
Within thee dwelt a haughty line that now go from their place;
Within thee fearless knights did dwell, who fought with mickle glee—
The enemies of proud Castile—the bane of Christentie!

'The mother of fair dames wert thou, of truth and beauty rare,
Into whose arms did courteous knights for solace sweet repair;
For whose dear sakes the gallants of Afric made display
Of might in joust and battle on many a bloody day.

'Here, gallants held it little thing for ladies' sake to die,
Or for the Prophet's honour, and pride of Soldanry;
For here did valour flourish, and deeds of warlike might
Ennobled lordly palaces in which was our delight.

'The gardens of thy Vega, its fields and blooming bowers—
Woe, woe! I see their beauty gone and scattered all their flowers!
No reverence can he claim—the King that such a land hath lost—
On charger never can he ride, nor be heard among the host;
But in some dark and dismal place, where none his face may see,
There, weeping and lamenting, alone that king should be.'—

Thus spake Granada's King as he was riding to the sea,
About to cross Gibraltar's Strait away to Barbary:
Thus he in heaviness of soul unto his Queen did cry—
(He had stopped and ta'en her in his arms, for together they did fly.)

' Unhappy King ! whose craven soul can brook' (she 'gan reply)
' To leave behind Granada—who hast not heart to die !—
Now for the love I bore thy youth, thee gladly could I slay—
For what is life to leave when such a crown is cast away ?'

THE DEATH OF DON ALONZO OF AGUILAR.

[THE Catholic zeal of Ferdinand and Isabella was gratified by the external
conversion at least of a great part of the Moors of Granada ; but the inhabit-
ants of the Sierra of Alpuxarra, a ridge of mountainous territory at no great
distance from that city, resisted every argument of the priests who were sent
among them, so that the royal order for Baptism was at length enforced by
arms.   The mountaineers held out for a time in several of their strong-
holds ; but were at last subdued, and nearly extirpated.   Among many
severe losses sustained by the Spanish in the course of this hill warfare,
none was more grievous than that recorded in the following ballad.   Don
Alonzo of Aguilar was the oldest brother of that Gonsalvo Hernandes y
Cordova of Aguilar who became so illustrious as to acquire the name of the
GREAT CAPTAIN.   This tragic story has been rendered familiar to all English
readers by the Bishop of Dromore's exquisite version of ' Rio Verde, Rio
Verde !']

FERNANDO, King of Arragon, before Granada lies,
With dukes and barons many a one, and champions of emprise ;
With all the captains of Castile that serve his lady's crown,
He drives Boabdil from his gates, and plucks the crescent down.

The cross is reared upon the towers, for our Redeemer's sake :
The King assembles all his powers, his triumph to partake ;
Yet at the royal banquet, there's trouble in his eye :—
' Now speak thy wish, it shall be done, great King !' the lordlings cry

Then spake Fernando—'Hear, grandees! which of ye all will go,
And give my banner in the breeze of Alpuxar to blow?
Those heights along the Moors are strong; now who, by dawn of day
Will plant the cross their cliffs among, and drive the dogs away?'

Then champion on champion high, and count on count doth look;
And faltering is the tongue of lord, and pale the cheek of duke;
Till starts up brave Alonzo, the knight of Aguilar,
The lowmost at the royal board, but foremost still in war.

And thus he speaks :—'I pray, my lord, that none but I may go;
For I made promise to the Queen, your consort, long ago,
That ere the war should have an end, I, for her royal charms
And for my duty to her grace, would show some feat of arms!'

Much joyed the King these words to hear—he bids Alonzo speed;
And long before their revel's o'er the knight is on his steed;
Alonzo's on his milk-white steed, with horsemen in his train,
A thousand horse, a chosen band, ere dawn the hills to gain.

They ride along the darkling ways, they gallop all the night;
They reach Nevada ere the cock hath harbingered the light—
But ere they've climbed that steep ravine, the east is glowing red,
And the Moors their lances bright have seen, and Christian banners spread.

Beyond the sands, between the rocks, where the old cork-trees grow,
The path is rough, and mounted men must singly march and slow;
There, o'er the path, the heathen range their ambuscado's line—
High up they wait for Aguilar, as the day begins to shine.

There nought avails the eagle-eye, the guardian of Castile,
The eye of wisdom, nor the heart that fear might never feel,
The arm of strength that wielded well the strong mace in the fray,
Nor the broad plate from whence the edge of falchion glanced away.

Not knightly valour there avails, nor skill of horse and spear ;
For rock on rock comes rumbling down from cliff and cavern drear ;
Down—down like driving hail they come, and horse and horsemen die
Like cattle whose despair is dumb when the fierce lightnings fly.

Alonzo, with a handful more, escapes into the field,
There, like a lion, stands at bay, in vain besought to yield ;
A thousand foes around are seen, but none draws near to fight ;
Afar, with bolt and javelin, they pierce the steadfast knight.

A hundred and a hundred darts are hissing round his head—
Had Aguilar a thousand hearts, their blood had all been shed ;
Faint and more faint he staggers upon the slippery sod—
At last his back is to the earth, he gives his soul to God.

With that the Moors plucked up their hearts to gaze upon his face,
And caitiffs mangled where he lay the scourge of Afric's race.
To woody Oxijera then the gallant corpse they drew,
And there upon the village-green they laid him out to view.

Upon the village-green he lay, as the moon was shining clear,
And all the village damsels to look on him drew near—
They stood around him all a-gaze, beside the big oak-tree,
And much his beauty they did praise, though mangled sore was he.

Now, so it fell, a Christian dame, that knew Alonzo well,
Not far from Oxijera did as a captive dwell,
And hearing all the marvels, across the woods came she,
To look upon this Christian corpse, and wash it decently.

She looked upon him, and she knew the face of Aguilar,
Although his beauty was disgraced with many a ghastly scar ;
She knew him, and she cursed the dogs that pierced him from afar,
And mangled him when he was slain—the Moors of Alpuxar.

The Moorish maidens while she spake, around her silence kept,
But her master dragged the dame away—then loud and long they wept ;
They washed the blood, with many a tear, from dint of dart and arrow,
And buried him near the waters clear of the brook of Alpuxarra.

THE DEPARTURE OF KING SEBASTIAN.

[THE reader is acquainted with the melancholy story of Sebastian, King of Portugal.
It was in 1578, that his unfortunate expedition and death took place
The following is a version of one of the Spanish ballads founded on the
history of Sebastian. There is another, which describes his death, almost in
the words of a ballad already translated, concerning King Juan I of Castile]

It was a Lusitanian lady, and she was lofty in degree,
Was fairer none nor nobler in all the realm than she ;
I saw her that her eyes were red, as, from her balcony,
They wandered o'er the crowded shore and the resplendent sea.

Gorgeous and gay, in Lisbon's Bay, with streamers flaunting wide,
Upon the gleaming waters Sebastian's galleys ride ;
His valorous armada (was never nobler sight !)
Hath young Sebastian marshalled against the Moorish might.

The breeze comes forth from the clear north, a gallant breeze there blows ;
Their sails they lift, then out they drift, and first Sebastian goes.
' May none withstand Sebastian's hand—God shield my King !' she said ;
Yet pale was that fair lady's cheek—her weeping eyes were red.

She looks on all the parting host, in all its pomp arrayed—
Each pennon on the wind is tost, each cognizance displayed ;
Each lordly galley flings abroad, above its armed prow,
The banner of the cross of God upon the breeze to flow.

But one there is, whose banner, above the Cross divine,
A scarf upholds, with azure folds, of love and faith the sign ;
Upon that galley's stern ye see a peerless warrior stand—
Though first he goes, still back he throws his eye upon the land.

Albeit through tears she looks, yet well may she that form descry—
Was never seen a vassal mien so noble and so high.
Albeit the lady's cheek was pale, albeit her eyes were red—
' May none withstand my true love's hand ! God bless my knight!' she said

There are a thousand barons, all harnessed cap-a-pee,
With helm and spear that glitter clear above the dark-green sea ;
No lack of gold or silver, to stamp each proud device
On shield or surcoat—nor of chains and jewellery of price.

The seamen's cheers the lady hears, and mingling voices come
From every deck, of glad rebeck, of trumpet, and of drum ;—
' Who dare withstand Sebastian's hand ?—what Moor his gage may fling
At young Sebastian's feet ?' she said.—' The Lord hath blessed my King.

GORGEOUS AND GAY, IN LISBON'S BAY, SEBASTIAN'S GALLEYS RIDE

MOORISH BALLADS.

It is sometimes difficult to determine which of the Moorish Ballads ought to be included in the Historical, which in the Romantic class; and for this reason, the following five specimens are placed by themselves. Several Ballads, decidedly of Moorish origin, such as REDUAN's VOW, THE FLIGHT FROM GRANADA, &c., have been printed in the preceding Section.

THE BULL-FIGHT OF GAZUL.

[GAZUL is the name of one of the Moorish heroes who figure in the *Historia de las Guerras Civiles de Granada.* The following ballad is one of very many in which the dexterity of the Moorish cavaliers in the Bull-fight is described. The reader will observe that the shape, activity, and resolution of the unhappy animal destined to furnish the amusement of the spectators, are enlarged upon—just as the qualities of a race-horse might be among ourselves: nor is the bull without his *name.* The day of the Baptist is a festival among the Mussulmans as well as among Christians.]

King ALMANZOR of Granada, he hath bid the trumpet sound,
He hath summoned all the Moorish lords from the hills and plains around;
From Vega and Sierra, from Betis and Xenil,
They have come with helm and cuirass of gold and twisted steel.

'Tis the holy Baptist's feast they hold in royalty and state,
And they have closed the spacious lists beside the Alhambra's gate;
In gowns of black with silver laced, within the tented ring,
Eight Moors to fight the bull are placed, in presence of the King.

Eight Moorish lords of valour tried, with stalwart arm and true
The onset of the beasts abide, as they come rushing through;
The deeds they've done, the spoils they've won, fill all with hope and trust—
Yet, ere high in heaven appears the sun, they all have bit the dust.

Then sounds the trumpet clearly, then clangs the loud tambour—
'Make room, make room for Gazul!—throw wide, throw wide the door!
Blow, blow the trumpet clearer still—more loudly strike the drum!
The Alcaydé of Algava to fight the bull doth come.'

And first before the King he passed, with reverence stooping low,
And next he bowed him to the Queen, and the Infantas all a-rowe;
Then to his lady's grace he turned, and she to him did throw
A scarf from out her balcony was whiter than the snow.

With the life-blood of the slaughtered lords all slippery is the sand,
Yet proudly in the centre hath Gazul ta'en his stand;
And ladies look with heaving breast, and lords with anxious eye,
But firmly he extends his arm—his look is calm and high.

Three bulls against the knight are loosed, and two come roaring on
He rises high in stirrup, forth stretching his rejón;
Each furious beast, upon the breast he deals him such a blow,
He blindly totters and gives back across the sand to go.

'Turn, Gazul—turn!' the people cry—the third comes up behind,
Low to the sand his head holds he, his nostrils snuff the wind;—
The mountaineers that lead the steers without stand whispering low,
'Now thinks this proud Alcaydé to stun Harpado so!'

From Guadiana comes he not, he comes not from Xenil,
From Guadalarif of the plain, or Barves of the hill;
But where from out the forest burst Xarama's waters clear,
Beneath the oak-trees was he nursed—this proud and stately steer.

Dark is his hide on either side, but the blood within doth boil,
And the dun hide glows, as if on fire, as he paws to the turmoil.
His eyes are jet, and they are set in crystal rings of snow ;
But now they stare with one red glare of brass upon the foe.

Upon the forehead of the bull the horns stand close and near,
From out the broad and wrinkled skull like daggers th. y appear ;
His neck is massy, like the trunk of some old knotted tree,
Whereon the monster's shagged mane, like billows curled, ye see.

His legs are short, his hams are thick, his hoofs are black as night,
Like a strong flail he holds his tail in fierceness of his might ;
Like something molten out of iron, or hewn from forth the rock,
Harpado of Xarama stands, to bide the Alcaydó's shock.

Now stops the drum ; close, close they come ; thrice meet, and thrice give back ;
The white foam of Harpado lies on the charger's breast of black—
The white foam of the charger on Harpado's front of dun ;—
Once more advance upon his lance—once more, thou fearless one !

Once more, once more !—in dust and gore to ruin must thou reel !—.
In vain, in vain thou tearest the sand with furious heel—
In vain, in vain, thou noble beast !—I see, I see thee stagger,
Now keen and cold thy neck must hold the stern Alcaydó's dagger !

They have slipped a noose around his feet, six horses are brought in,
And away they drag Harpado with a loud and joyful din.
Now stoop thee, lady, from thy stand, and the ring of price bestow
Upon Gazul of Algava, that hath laid Harpado low.

THE ZEGRI'S BRIDE.

[THE reader cannot need to be reminded of the fatal effects which were produced by the feuds subsisting between the two great families, or rather races, of the Zegris and the Abencerrages of Granada. This ballad is also from the *Guerras Civiles.*]

OF all the blood of Zegri, the chief is Lisaro,
To wield rejón like him is none, or javelin to throw ;
From the place of his dominion, he ere the dawn doth go,
From Alcala de Henares, he rides in weed of woe.

He rides not now as he was wont when ye have seen him speed
To the field of gay Toledo, to fling his lusty reed ;
No gambeson of silk is on, nor rich embroidery
Of gold-wrought robe or turban, nor jewelled tahali.

No amethyst nor garnet is shining on his brow,
No crimson sleeve, which damsels weave at Tunis, decks him now ;
The belt is black, the hilt is dim, but the sheathed blade is bright ;
They have housened his barb in a murky garb, but yet her hoofs are light.

Four horsemen good, of the Zegri blood, with Lisaro go out ;
No flashing spear may tell them near, but yet their shafts are stout ;
In darkness and in swiftness rides every armed knight—
The foam on the rein ye may see it plain, but nothing else is white.

G

Young Lisaro, as on they go, his bonnet doffeth he—
Between its folds a sprig it holds of a dark and glossy tree;
That sprig of bay, were it away, right heavy heart had he—
Fair Zayda to her Zegri gave that token privily.

And ever as they rode, he looked upon his lady's boon—
' God knows,' quoth he, ' what fate may be !—I may be slaughtered soon;
Thou still art mine, though scarce the sign of hope that bloomed whilere,
But in my grave I yet shall have my Zayda's token dear.'

Young Lisaro was musing so, when onwards on the path
He well could see them riding slow—then pricked he in his wrath :—
The raging sire, the kinsmen of Zayda's hateful house,
Fought well that day, yet in the fray the Zegri won his spouse.

THE BRIDAL OF ANDALLA.

' Rise up, rise up, Xarifa ! lay the golden cushion down ;
Rise up, come to the window, and gaze with all the town !
From gay guitar and violin the silver notes are flowing,
And the lovely lute doth speak between the trumpet's lordly blowing,
And banners bright from lattice light are waving every where,
And the tall tall plume of our cousin's bridegroom floats proudly in the air.
Rise up, rise up, Xarifa ! lay the golden cushion down ;
Rise up, come to the window, and gaze with all the town !

' Arise, arise, Xarifa ! I see Andalla's face—
He bends him to the people with a calm and princely grace ;

THE BRIDAL OF ANDALLA.

Page 82.

Through all the land of Xeres and banks of Guadalquiver
Rode forth bridegroom so brave as he, so brave and lovely never.
Yon tall plume waving o'er his brow, of purple mixed with white,
I guess 'twas wreathed by Zara, whom he will wed to-night.
Rise up, rise up, Xarifa! lay the golden cushion down;
Rise up, come to the window, and gaze with all the town!

'What aileth thee, Xarifa—what makes thine eyes look down?
Why stay ye from the window far, nor gaze with all the town?
I've heard you say on many a day, and sure you said the truth,
Andalla rides without a peer among all Granada's youth:
Without a peer he rideth, and yon milk-white horse doth go
Beneath his stately master, with a stately step and slow :—
Then rise—oh! rise, Xarifa, lay the golden cushion down;
Unseen here through the lattice, you may gaze with all the town!'

The Zegri lady rose not, nor laid her cushion down,
Nor came she to the window to gaze with all the town;
But though her eyes dwelt on her knee, in vain her fingers strove,
And though her needle pressed the silk, no flower Xarifa wove;
One bonny rose-bud she had traced before the noise drew nigh—
That bonny bud a tear effaced, slow drooping from her eye—
'No—no!' she sighs—'bid me not rise, nor lay my cushion down,
To gaze upon Andalla with all the gazing town!'

'Why rise ye not, Xarifa—nor lay your cushion down—
Why gaze ye not, Xarifa—with all the gazing town?
Hear, hear the trumpet how it swells, and how the people cry:
He stops at Zara's palace-gate—why sit ye still—oh, why!'
——'At Zara's gate stops Zara's mate; in him shall I discover
The dark-eyed youth pledged me his truth with tears, and was my lover!
I will not rise, with weary eyes, nor lay my cushion down,
To gaze on false Andalla with all the gazing town!'

G 2

ZARA'S EAR-RINGS.

My ear-rings! my ear-rings! they've dropped into the well,
And what to say to Muça, I cannot, cannot tell—
'Twas thus, Granada's fountain by, spoke Albuharez' daughter:—
The well is deep—far down they lie, beneath the cold blue water;
To me did Muça give them, when he spoke his sad farewell,
And what to say when he comes back, alas! I cannot tell.

My ear-rings! my ear-rings!—they were pearls, in silver set,
That, when my Moor was far away, I ne'er should him forget;
That I ne'er to other tongues should list, nor smile on other's tale,
But remember he my lips had kissed, pure as those ear-rings pale.
When he comes back, and hears that I have dropped them in the well,
Oh! what will Muça think of me!—I cannot, cannot tell!

My ear-rings! my ear-rings!—he'll say they should have been,
Not of pearl and of silver, but of gold and glittering sheen,
Of jasper and of onyx, and of diamond shining clear,
Changing to the changing light, with radiance insincere;
That changeful mind unchanging gems are not befitting well;
Thus will he think—and what to say, alas! I cannot tell.

He'll think, when I to market went I loitered by the way;
He'll think a willing ear I lent to all the lads might say;
He'll think some other lover's hand, among my tresses noosed,
From the ears where he had placed them my rings of pearl unloosed;
He'll think when I was sporting so beside this marble well
My pearls fell in—and what to say, alas! I cannot tell.
He'll say, I am a woman, and we are all the same; ·
He'll say, I loved, when he was here to whisper of his flame—

ZARA'S EAR-RINGS

THE LAMENTATION FOR CELIN

Page 85.

But, when he went to Tunis, my virgin troth had broken,
And thought no more of Muça, and cared not for his token.
My ear-rings ! my ear-rings : oh ! luckless, luckless well,—
For what to say to Muça—alas ! I cannot tell.

I'll tell the truth to Muça—and I hope he will believe—
That I thought of him at morning, and thought of him at eve :
That, musing on my lover, when down the sun was gone,
His ear-rings in my hand I held, by the fountain all alone ;
And that my mind was o'er the sea, when from my hand they fell,
And that deep his love lies in my heart, as they lie in the well.

THE LAMENTATION FOR CELIN.

At the gate of old Granada, when all its bolts are barred,
At twilight, at the Vega-gate, there is a trampling heard ;
There is a trampling heard, as of horses treading slow,
And a weeping voice of women, and a heavy sound of woe.
What tower is fallen, what star is set, what chief come these bewailing ?—
' A tower is fallen, a star is set !—Alas ! alas for Celin ! '

Three times they knock, three times they cry—and wide the doors they
Dejectedly they enter, and mournfully they go ;   [throw ;
In gloomy lines they mustering stand beneath the hollow porch,
Each horseman grasping in his hand a black and flaming torch ;
Wet is each eye as they go by, and all around is wailing,
For all have heard the misery.—' Alas ! alas for Celin ! '
Him, yesterday, a Moor did slay, of Bencerraje's blood—
'Twas at the solemn jousting—around the nobles stood ;
The nobles of the land were by, and ladies bright and fair
Looked from their latticed windows, the haughty sight to share ;

But now the nobles all lament—the ladies are bewailing—
For he was Granada's darling knight.—'Alas! alas for Celin!'

Before him ride his vassals, in order two by two,
With ashes on their turbans spread, most pitiful to view;
Behind him his four sisters, each wrapped in sable veil,
Between the tambour's dismal strokes take up their doleful tale;
When stops the muffled drum, ye hear their brotherless bewailing,
And all the people, far and near, cry—'Alas! alas for Celin!'

Oh! lovely lies he on the bier, above the purple pall,
The flower of all Granada's youth, the loveliest of them all;
His dark, dark eyes are closed, his rosy lip is pale,
The crust of blood lies black and dim upon his burnished mail;
And ever more the hoarse tambour breaks in upon their wailing—
Its sound is like no earthly sound—'Alas! alas for Celin!'

The Moorish maid at the lattice stands—the Moor stands at his door;
One maid is wringing of her hands, and one is weeping sore;
Down to the dust men bow their heads, and ashes black they strew
Upon their broidered garments, of crimson, green, and blue;
Before each gate the bier stands still—then bursts the loud bewailing
From door and lattice, high and low—'Alas! alas for Celin!'

An old old woman cometh forth, when she hears the people cry—
Her hair is white as silver, like horn her glazed eye:
'Twas she that nursed him at her breast—that nursed him long ago:
She knows not whom they all lament, but soon she well shall know!
With one deep shriek, she thro' doth break, when her ears receive their
    wailing—
Let me kiss my Celin ere I die—'Alas! alas for Celin!'

THE MOOR CALAYNOS.

[In the following version, I have taken liberty to omit many of the introductory
stanzas of the famous *Coplas de Calainos.* The reader will remember that this
ballad is alluded to in Don Quixote, where the knight's nocturnal visit to
Toboso is described. It is generally believed to be among the most ancient, and
certainly was among the most popular, of all the ballads in the Cancionero.]

'I HAD six Moorish nurses, but the seventh was not a Moor—
The Moors they gave me milk enow, but the Christian gave me lore;
And she told me ne'er to listen, though sweet the words might be,
Till he that spake had proved his troth, and pledged a gallant fee.'

'Fair damsel,' quoth Calaynos, 'if thou wilt go with me,
Say what may win thy favour, and mine that gift shall be :
Fair stands the castle on the rock, the city in the vale,
And bonny is the red red gold, and rich the silver pale.'

'Fair sir,' quoth she, 'virginity I never will lay down
For gold, nor yet for silver, for castle, nor for town ;
But I will be your leman for the heads of certain peers—
And I ask but three—Rinaldo's, Roland's, and Olivier's.'

He kissed her hand where she did stand, he kissed her lips also,
And 'Bring forth,' he cries, 'my pennon, for to Paris I must go !'—
I wot he saw them rearing his banner broad right soon,
Whereon revealed his bloody field its pale and crescent moon.

That broad bannere the Moor did rear, ere many days were gone,
In foul disdain of Charlemagne, by the church of good Saint John;
In the midst of stately Paris, on the royal banks of Seine,
Shall never scornful Paynim that pennon rear again.

His banner he hath planted high, and loud his trumpet blown,
That all the twelve might hear it well around King Charles's throne;
The note he blew right well they know; both paladin and peer
Had the trumpet heard of that stern lord in many a fierce career.

It chanced the King, that fair morning, to the chase had made him bowne,
With many a knight of warlike might and prince of high renown :
Sir Reynold of Montalban, and Claros' lord, Gaston,
Behind him rode, and Bertram good, that reverend old baron.

Black D'Ardennes' eye of mastery in that proud troop was seen ;
And there was Urgel's giant force, and Guarinos' princely mien ;
Gallant and gay upon that day was Baldwin's youthful cheer,
But first did ride, by Charles's side, Roland and Olivier.

Now in a ring, around the King, not far in the greenwood,
Awaiting all the huntsman's call, it chanced the nobles stood ;
'Now list, mine earls, now list !' quoth Charles—'yon breeze will come
　　again—
Some trumpet-note methinks doth float from the fair bank of Seine.'

He scarce had heard the trumpet, the word he scarce had said,
When among the trees he near him sees a dark and turbaned head—
'Now stand, now stand at my command, bold Moor !' quoth Charlemagne,
'That turban green, how dare it be seen among the woods of Seine ?'

'My turban green must needs be seen among the woods of Seine,'
The Moor replied, 'since here I ride in quest of Charlemagne ;
For I serve the Moor Calaynos, and I his defiance bring
To every lord that sits at the board of Charlemagne your King.

' Now lordlings fair, if any where in the wood ye've seen him riding,
Oh, tell me plain the path he has ta'en—there is no cause for chiding—
For my lord hath blown his trumpet by every gate of Paris,
Long hours in vain, by the bank of Seine, upon his steed he tarries.'

When the Emperor had heard the Moor, full red was his old cheek:
' Go back, base cur, upon the spur, for I am he you seek :—
Go back, and tell your master to commend him to Mahoun,
For his soul shall dwell with him in hell, or ere yon sun go down !

' Mine arm is weak, my hairs are gray '—(thus spake King Charlemagne'
' Would for one hour I had the power of my young days again,
As when I plucked the Saxon from out the mountain-den—
Oh, soon should cease the vaunting of this proud Saracen !

' Though now mine arm be weakened, though now my hairs be gray,
The hard-won praise of other days cannot be swept away ;
If shame there be, my liegemen, that shame on you must lie ;
Go forth, go forth, good Roland ; to-night this Moor must die !'

Then out and spake rough Roland—' Ofttimes I've thinned the ranks
Of the hot Moor, and when 'twas o'er have won me little thanks ;
Some carpet knight will take delight to do this doughty feat,
Whom damsels gay shall well repay with smiles and whispers sweet.'

Then out and spake Sir Baldwin—the youngest peer was he—
The youngest and the comeliest—' Let none go forth but me ;
Sir Roland is mine uncle, and he may in safety jeer,
But I will show, the youngest may be Sir Roland's peer.'

' Nay, go not thou,' quoth Charlemagne, ' thou art my gallant youth,
And braver none I look upon ; but thy cheek it is too smooth,
And the curls upon thy forehead they are too glossy bright :
Some elder peer must couch his spear against this crafty knight.'

But away, away goes Baldwin—no words can stop him now;
Behind him lies the greenwood, he hath gained the mountain's brow;
He reineth first his charger, within the church-yard green,
Where, striding slow the elms below, the haughty Moor is seen.

Then out and spake Calaynos—' Fair youth, I greet thee well;
Thou art a comely stripling, and if thou with me wilt dwell,
All for the grace of thy sweet face, thou shalt not lack thy fee,
Within my lady's chamber a pretty page thou'lt be.'

An angry man was Baldwin when thus he heard him speak :
' Proud knight,' quoth he, ' I come with thee a bloody spear to break ! '
Oh, sternly smiled Calaynos, when thus he heard him say :
Oh, loudly as he mounted his mailed barb did neigh.

One shout, one thrust, and in the dust young Baldwin lies full low;
No youthful knight could bear the might of that fierce warrior's blow;
Calaynos draws his falchion, and waves it to and fro :
' Thy name now say, and for mercy pray, or to hell thy soul must go ! '

The helpless youth revealed the truth : then said the conquerour -
' I spare thee for thy tender years, and for thy great valour :—
But thou must rest thee captive here, and serve me on thy knee,
For fain I'd tempt some doughtier peer to come and rescue thee.

Sir Roland heard that haughty word—(he stood behind the wall) —
His heart, I trow, was heavy enow, when he saw his kinsman fall,
But now his heart was burning, and never word he said,
But clasped his buckler on his arm, his helmet on his head.

Another sight saw the Moorish knight, when Roland blew his horn
To call him to the combat in anger and in scorn;
All cased in steel from head to heel, in the stirrup high he stood,
The long spear quivered in his hand, as if athirst for blood.

Then out and spake Calaynos :—'Thy name I fain would hear ;
A coronet on thy helm is set ; I guess thou art a peer.'—
Sir Roland lifted up his horn, and blew another blast :
'No words, base Moor !' quoth Roland, 'this hour shall be thy last !'

I wot they met full swiftly, I wot the shock was rude ;
Down fell the misbeliever, and o'er him Roland stood ;
Close to his throat the steel he brought, and plucked his beard full sore :
'What devil brought thee hither?—speak out or die, false Moor !'

'Oh ! I serve a noble damsel, a haughty maid of Spain,
And in evil day I took my way, that I her grace might gain ;
For every gift I offered my lady did disdain,
And craved the ears of certain peers that ride with Charlemagne.'

Then loudly laughed rough Roland :—'Full few will be her tears,
It was not love her soul did move, who bade thee beard THE PEERS'—
With that he smote upon his throat, and spurned his crest in twain ;
'No more,' he cries, 'this moon will rise above the woods of Seine !'

THE ESCAPE OF GAYFEROS.

[The story of Gayfer de Bourdeaux is to be found at great length in the Romantic
Chronicle of Charlemagne ; and it has supplied the Spanish minstrels with subjects for a long series of ballads. In that which follows, Gayferos, yet a boy, is
represented as hearing from his mother the circumstances of his father's death ;
and as narrowly escaping with his own life, in consequence of his step-father,
Count Galvan's cruelty.

There is another ballad which represents Gayferos, now grown to be a man, as
coming in the disguise of a pilgrim to his mother's house, and slaying his step-
father with his own hand. The Countess is only satisfied as to his identity by
the circumstance of the finger :—

> "El dedo bien es aqueste, aqui lo vereys faltar:
> La condesa que esto oyera empezole de abraçar.]

Before her knee the boy did stand, within the dais so fair,
The golden shears were in her hand, to clip his curled hair ;
And ever, as she clipped the curls, such doleful words she spake,
That tears ran from Gayferos' eyes, for his sad mother's sake.

'God grant a beard were on thy face, and strength thine arm within,
To fling a spear, or swing a mace, like Roland Paladin !
For then, I think, thou wouldst avenge thy father that is dead,
Whom envious traitors slaughtered within thy mother's bed ;

'Their bridal-gifts were rich and rare, that hate might not be seen ;
They cut me garments broad and fair—none fairer hath the Queen.'—
Then out and spake the little boy—'Each night to God I call,
And to his blessed Mother, to make me strong and tall.'

The Count he heard Gayferos, in the palace where he lay:
'Now silence, silence, Countess! it is falsehood that you say—
I neither slew the man, nor hired another's sword to slay;
But for that the mother hath desired, be sure the son shall pay!'

The Count called to his esquires—(old followers were they,
Whom the dead lord had nurtured for many a merry day)—
He bade them take their old lord's heir, and stop his tender breath;
Alas! 'twas piteous but to hear the manner of that death.

'List, esquires, list, for my command is offspring of mine oath,
The stirrup-foot and the hilt-hand see that ye sunder both;
That ye cut out his eyes 'twere best—the safer he will go;
And bring a finger and the heart, that I his end may know.'

The esquires took the little boy aside with them to go;
Yet, as they went, they did repent—'O God! must this be so?
How shall we think to look for grace, if this poor child we slay,
When ranged before Christ Jesu's face at the great judgment-day?'

While they, not knowing what to do, were standing in such talk,
The Countess' little lap-dog bitch by chance did cross their walk;
Then out and spake one of the 'squires (you may hear the words he said)
'I think the coming of this bitch may serve us in good stead:—

'Let us take out the bitch's heart, and give it to Galvan;
The boy may with a finger part, and be no worser man.'—
With that they cut the joint away, and whispered in his ear,
That he must wander many a day, nor once those parts come near.

'Your uncle grace and love will show; he is a bounteous man.'
And so they let Gayferos go, and turned them to Galvan;
The heart and the small finger upon the board they laid,
And of Gayferos' slaughter a cunning story made

The Countess, when she hears them, in great grief loudly cries:
Meantime the stripling safely unto his uncle hies :—
'Now welcome, my fair boy,' he said, 'what good news may they be
Come with thee to thine uncle's hall ?'—'Sad tidings come with me : -

'The false Galvan had laid his plan to have me in my grave;
But I've escaped him, and am here, my boon from thee to crave—
Rise up, rise up, mine uncle, thy brother's blood they've shed !
Rise up—they've slain my father within my mother's bed !'

MELISENDRA.

[THIS is a version of another of the ballads concerning Gayferos. It is quoted in the chapter of the Puppet-show in Don Quixote. 'Now, sirs, he that you see there a horse-back, wrapt up in the Gascoign-cloak, is Don Gayferos himself, whom his wife, now revenged on the Moor for his impudence, seeing from the battlements of the tower, takes for a stranger, and talks with him as such, according to the ballad—

Quoth Melisendra, if perchance,
Sir Traveller, you go for France, &c.

The place of the lady's captivity was Saragossa, anciently called Sansueña.]

At Sansueña, in the tower, fair Melisendra lies,
Her heart is far away in France, and tears are in her eyes;
The twilight shade is thickening laid on Sansueña's plain,
Yet wistfully the lady her weary eyes doth strain.

She gazes from the dungeon strong, forth on the road to Paris,
Weeping and wondering why so long her lord Gayferos tarries;
When lo ! a knight appears in view—a knight of Christian mien :
Upon a milk-white charger he rides the elms between.

She from her window reaches forth her hand a sign to make :
' Oh, if you be a knight of worth, draw near for mercy's sake ;
For mercy and sweet charity, draw near, Sir Knight, to me,
And tell me if ye ride to France, or whither bowne ye be—

' Oh, if ye be a Christian knight, and if to France you go,
I pray thee tell Gayferos that you have seen my woe ;
That you have seen me weeping, here in the Moorish tower,
While he is gay by night and day in hall and lady's bower.

' Seven summers have I waited—seven winters long are spent :
Yet word of comfort none he speaks, nor token hath he sent ;
And if he is weary of my love, and would have me wed a stranger,
Still say his love is true to him—nor time nor wrong can change her !'

The knight on stirrup rising, bids her wipe her tears away :
' My love, no time for weeping, no peril save delay ;
Come, boldly spring, and lightly leap—no listening Moor is near us,
And by dawn of day we'll be far away : '—so spake the knight Gayferos.

She hath made the sign of the Cross divine, and an Avé she hath said,
And she dares the leap both wide and deep—that lady without dread ;
And he hath kissed her pale pale cheek, and lifted her behind :
Saint Denis speed the milk-white steed !—no Moor their path shall find.

LADY ALDA'S DREAM.

[The following is an attempt to render one of the most admired of all the
Spanish ballads.

> En Paris esta Dona Alda, la esposa de Don Roldan,
> Trecientas damas con ella, para la acompañar,
> Todas visten un vestido, todas calzan un calzar, &c.

In its whole structure and strain, it bears a very remarkable resemblance
to several of our own ballads, both English and Scottish.]

In Paris sits the lady that shall be Sir Roland's bride,
Three hundred damsels with her, her bidding to abide;
All clothed in the same fashion, both the mantle and the shoon,
All eating at one table, within her hall at noon :
All, save the Lady Alda—she is lady of them all—
She keeps her place upon the dais, and they serve her in her hall ;
The thread of gold a hundred spin, the lawn a hundred weave,
And a hundred play sweet melody within Alda's bower at eve.

With the sound of their sweet playing, the lady falls asleep,
And she dreams a doleful dream, and her damsels hear her weep :
There is sorrow in her slumber, and she waketh with a cry,
And she calleth for her damsels, and swiftly they come nigh.
'Now what is it, Lady Alda—(you may hear the words they say)—
'Bringeth sorrow to thy pillow, and chaseth sleep away?'
'Oh, my maidens !' quoth the lady, 'my heart it is full sore—
I have dreamt a dream of evil, and can slumber never more :

'For I was upon a mountain, in a bare and desert place,
And I saw a mighty eagle, and a falcon he did chase ;
And to me the falcon came, and I hid it in my breast ;
But the mighty bird, pursuing, came and rent away my vest ;
And he scattered all the feathers, and blood was on his beak,
And over, as he tore and tore, I heard the falcon shriek.
Now read my vision, damsels—now read my dream to me,
For my heart may well be heavy that doleful sight to see.'

Out spake the foremost damsel was in her chamber there—
(You may hear the words she says)—' Oh ! my lady's dream is fair :
The mountain is St. Denis' choir, and thou the falcon art ;
And the eagle strong that teareth the garment from thy heart,
And scattereth the feathers, he is the Paladin,
That, when again he comes from Spain, must sleep thy bower within.
Then be blythe of cheer, my lady, for the dream thou must not grieve,
It means but that thy bridegroom shall come to thee at eve.'

' If thou hast read my vision, and read it cunningly,'
Thus said the Lady Alda, ' thou shalt not lack thy fee.'—
But woe is me for Alda ! there was heard, at morning hour,
A voice of lamentation within that lady's bower ;
For there had come to Paris a messenger by night,
And his horse it was a-weary, and his visage it was white ;
And there's weeping in the chamber, and there's silence in the hall,
For Sir Roland has been slaughtered in the chase of Roncesval.

THE ADMIRAL GUARINOS.

[This is the ballad which Don Quixote and Sancho Panza, when at Toboso, over-
heard a peasant singing, as he was going to his work at daybreak.]

The day of Roncesvalles was a dismal day for you,
Ye men of France, for there the lance of King Charles was broke in two:
Ye well may curse that rueful field, for many a noble peer
In fray or fight the dust did bite beneath Bernardo's spear.

There captured was Guarinos, King Charles's admiral;
Seven Moorish kings surrounded him, and seized him for their thrall;
Seven times, when all the chase was o'er, for Guarinos lots they cast,
Seven times Marlotes won the throw, and the knight was his at last.

Much joy had then Marlotes, and his captive much did prize;
Above all the wealth of Araby, he was precious in his eyes.
Within his tent at evening he made the best of cheer,
And thus, the banquet done, he spake unto his prisoner;

'Now, for the sake of Alla, Lord Admiral Guarinos,
Be thou a Moslem, and much love shall ever rest between us:
Two daughters have I—all the day thy handmaid one shall be,
The other (and the fairer far) by night shall cherish thee.

RONCEVAUX.

'The one shall be thy waiting-maid, thy weary feet to lave,
To scatter perfumes on thy head, and fetch thee garments brave;
The other—she the pretty—shall deck her bridal-bower,
And my field and my city they both shall be her dower;

'If more thou wishest, more I'll give; speak boldly what thy thought is.'
Thus earnestly and kindly to Guarinos said Marlotes:
But not a moment did he take to ponder or to pause,
Thus clear and quick the answer of the Christian captain was :—

'Now, God forbid! Marlotes, and Mary, his dear mother,
That I should leave the faith of Christ, and bind me to another:
For women—I've one wife in France, and I'll wed no more in Spain:
I change not faith, I break not vow, for courtesy or gain.'

Wroth waxed King Marlotes, when thus he heard him say,
And all for ire commanded, he should be led away;
Away unto the dungeon-keep, beneath its vault to lie,
With fetters bound in darkness deep, far off from sun and sky.

With iron bands they bound his hands : that sore unworthy plight
Might well express his helplessness, doomed never more to fight.
Again, from cincture down to knee, long bolts of iron he bore,
Which signified the knight should ride on charger never more.

Three times alone, in all the year, it is the captive's doom
To see God's daylight bright and clear, instead of dungeon-gloom;
Three times alone they bring him out, like Samson long ago,
Before the Moorish rabble-rout to be a sport and show.

On three high feasts they bring him forth, a spectacle to be—
The feast of Pasque, and the great day of the Nativity,
And on that morn, more solemn yet, when maidens strip the bowers,
And gladden mosque and minaret with the firstlings of the flowers.

Days come and go of gloom and show: seven years are come and gone;
And now doth fall the festival of the holy Baptist John;
Christian and Moslem tilts and jousts, to give it homage due,
And rushes on the paths to spread they force the sulky Jew.

Marlotes, in his joy and pride, a target high doth rear—
Below the Moorish knights must ride, and pierce it with the spear;
But 'tis so high up in the sky, albeit much they strain,
No Moorish lance so far may fly, Marlotes' prize to gain.

Wroth waxed King Marlotes, when he beheld them fail;
The whisker trembled on his lip—his cheek for ire was pale;
And heralds proclamation made, with trumpets, through the town—
'Nor child shall suck, nor man shall eat, till the mark be tumbled down.'

The cry of proclamation, and the trumpet's haughty sound,
Did send an echo to the vault where the Admiral was bound.
'Now, help me God!' the captive cries, 'what means this din so loud?
O Queen of Heaven! be vengeance given on these thy haters proud!

'Oh! is it that some Pagan gay doth Marlotes' daughter wed,
And that they bear my scorned fair in triumph to his bed?
Or is it that the day is come—one of the hateful three—
When they with trumpet, fife, and drum, make heathen game of me?'

These words the jailer chanced to hear, and thus to him he said—
'These tabors, Lord, and trumpets clear conduct no bride to bed;
Nor has the feast come round again, when he that has the right
Commands thee forth, thou foe of Spain, to glad the people's sight.

'This is the joyful morning of John the Baptist's day,
When Moor and Christian feasts at home, each in his nation's way;
But now our king commands that none his banquet shall begin,
Until some knight, by strength or sleight, the spearman's prize do win.'

Then out and spake Guarinos—'Oh! soon each man should feel,
Were I but mounted once again on my own gallant steed:
Oh! were I mounted as of old, and harnessed cap-a-pee,
Full soon Marlotes' prize I'd hold, whate'er its price may be!

'Give me my horse, mine old grey horse, so be he is not dead,
All gallantly caparisoned, with plate on breast and head,
And give the lance I brought from France; and if I win it not
My life shall be the forfeiture—I'll yield it on the spot.'

The jailer wondered at his words: thus to the knight said he—
'Seven weary years of chains and gloom have little humbled thee;
There's never a man in Spain, I trow, the like so well might bear
And if thou wilt, I with thy vow will to the King repair.'

The jailer put his mantle on, and came unto the King—
He found him sitting on the throne, within his listed ring;
Close to his ear he planted him, and the story did begin,
How bold Guarinos vaunted him the spearman's prize to win.

That, were he mounted but once more on his own gallant grey,
And armed with the lance he bore on Roncesvalles' day,
What never Moorish knight could pierce, he would pierce it at a blow,
Or give with joy his life-blood fierce, at Marlotes' feet to flow.

Much marvelling, then said the King—'Bring Sir Guarinos forth,
And in the grange go seek ye for his grey steed of worth;
His arms are rusty on the wall—seven years have gone, I judge,
Since that strong horse has bent his force to be a carrion drudge;

'Now this will be a sight indeed, to see the enfeebled lord
Essay to mount that ragged steed and draw that rusty sword—
And for the vaunting of his phrase he well deserves to die—
So, jailer, gird his harness on, and bring your champion nigh.'

They have girded on his shirt of mail, his cuisses well they've clasped,
And they've barred the helm on his visage pale, and his hand the lance hath
    grasped,
And they have caught the old grey horse, the horse he loved of yore,
And he stands pawing at the gate—caparisoned once more.

When the knight came out, the Moors did shout, and loudly laughed the
    King,
For the horse he pranced and capered, and furiously did fling;
But Guarinos whispered in his ear, and looked into his face—
Then stood the old charger like a lamb, with a calm and gentle grace.

Oh! lightly did Guarinos vault into the saddle-tree,
And slowly riding down made halt before Marlotes' knee;
Again the heathen laughed aloud—'All hail, sir knight,' quoth he,
'Now do thy best, thou champion proud: thy blood I look to see.'

With that, Guarinos, lance in rest, against the scoffer rode,
Pierced at one thrust his envious breast, and down his turban trode.
Now ride, now ride, Guarinos—nor lance nor rowel spare—
Slay, slay, and gallop for thy life: the land of France lies *there!*

THE LADY OF THE TREE

Page 165.

THE LADY OF THE TREE.

[THE following is one of the few old Spanish ballads in which mention is made
of the Fairies. The sleeping child's being taken away from the arms of
the nurse is a circumstance quite in accordance with our own tales of Fairy-
land; but the seven years' enchantment in the tree reminds us more
of those oriental fictions, the influence of which has stamped so many
indelible traces on the imaginative literature of Spain.]

THE knight had hunted long, and twilight closed the day,
His hounds were weak and weary—his hawk had flown away;
He stopped beneath an oak, an old and mighty tree,—
Then out the maiden spoke, and a comely maid was she.

The knight 'gan lift his eye the shady boughs between—
She had her seat on high among the oak-leaves green;
Her golden curls lay clustering above her breast of snow,
But when the breeze was westering, upon it they did flow.

'Oh, fear not, gentle knight! there is no cause for fear;
I am a good king's daughter, long years enchanted here;
Seven cruel fairies found me—they charmed a sleeping child—
Seven years their charm hath bound me, a damsel undefiled.

'Seven weary years are gone since o'er me charms they threw;
I have dwelt here alone—I have seen none but you.
My seven sad years are spent;—for Christ that died on rood,
Thou noble knight consent, and lead me from the wood:

'Oh, bring me forth again from out this darksome place--
I dare not sleep for terror of the unholy race.
Oh, take me, gentle sir! I'll be a wife to thee—
I'll be thy lowly leman, if wife I may not be!'

'Till dawns the morning, wait, thou lovely lady! here;
I'll ask my mother straight, for her reproof I fear.'
'Oh, ill beseems thee, knight!' said she, that maid forlorn,
'The blood of kings to slight—a lady's tears to scorn!'

He came when morning broke, to fetch the maid away,
But could not find the oak wherein she made her stay;
All through the wilderness he sought in bower and tree;—
Fair lordlings, well ye guess what weary heart had he.

There came a sound of voices from up the forest glen,
The King had come to find her with all his gentlemen;
They rode in mickle glee—a joyous cavalcade—
Fair in the midst rode she, but never word she said;

Though on the green he knelt, no look on him she cast:—
His hand was on the hilt ere all the train were past—
'Oh, shame to knightly blood! Oh, scorn to chivalry!
I'll die within the wood:—No eye my death shall see!

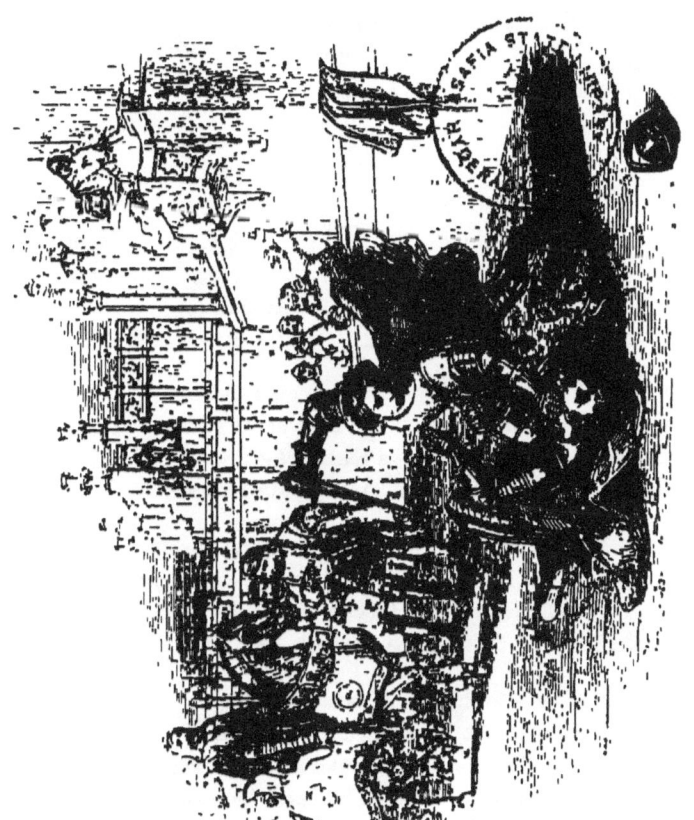

THE AVENGING CHILDE.

Page 107.

THE AVENGING CHILDE.

Hurrah! hurrah! avoid the way of the Avenging Childe;
His horse is swift as sands that drift—an Arab of the wild;
His gown is twisted round his arm—a ghastly cheek he wears;
And in his hand, for deadly harm, a hunting knife he bears.

Avoid that knife in battle-strife:—that weapon short and thin,
The dragon's gore hath bathed it o'er, seven times 'twas steeped therein;
Seven times the smith hath proved its pith—it cuts a coulter through;
In France the blade was fashioned—from Spain the shaft it drew.

He sharpens it, as he doth ride, upon his saddle bow—
He sharpens it on either side, he makes the steel to glow:
He rides to find Don Quadros, that false and faitour knight;
His glance of ire is hot as fire, although his cheek be white.

He found him standing by the King within the judgment-hall;
He rushed within the barons' ring—he stood before them all:
Seven times he gazed and pondered, if he the deed should do;
Eight times distraught he looked and thought—then out his dagger flew.

He stabbed therewith at Quadros:—the King did step between;
It pierced his royal garment of purple wove with green:
He fell beneath the canopy, upon the tiles he lay.
'Thou traitor keen, what dost thou mean?—thy King why wouldst thou slay?'

'Now, pardon, pardon,' cried the Childe, 'I stabbed not, King, at thee,
But him, that caitiff, blood-defiled, who stood beside thy knee;
Eight brothers were we—in the land might none more loving be—
They all are slain by Quadros' hand—they all are dead but me.

'Good King I fain would wash the stain—for vengeance is my cry;
This murderer with sword and spear to battle I defy!'—
But all took part with Quadros, except one lovely May—
Except the King's fair daughter, none word for him would say.

She took their hands, she led them forth into the court below;
She bade the ring be guarded—she bade the trumpet blow;
From lofty place for that stern race the signal she did throw:—
'With truth and right the Lord will fight—together let them go!'

The one is up, the other down: the hunter's knife is bare;
It cuts the lace beneath the face—it cuts through beard and hair;
Right soon that knife hath quenched his life, the head is sundered sheer;
Then gladsome smiled the Avenging Childe, and fixed it on his spear.

But when the King beholds him bring that token of his truth,
Nor scorn nor wrath his bosom hath:—' Kneel down, thou noble youth;
Kneel down, kneel down, and kiss my crown—I am no more thy foe;
My daughter now may pay the vow she plighted long ago!'

COUNT ARNALDOS.

[FROM the Cancionero of Antwerp, 1555. I suppose some religious
allegory is intended.]

WHO had ever such adventure,
    Holy priest, or virgin nun,
As befel the Count Arnaldos
    At the rising of the sun?

On his wrist the hawk was hooded,
    Forth with horn and hound went he.
When he saw a stately galley
    Sailing on the silent sea.

Sail of satin, masts of cedar,
    Burnished poop of beaten gold—
Many a morn you'll hood your falcon
    Ere you such a bark behold.

Sails of satin, masts of cedar,
    Golden poops may come again,
But 'mortal ear no more shall listen
    To yon grey-haired sailor's strain.

Heart may beat, and eye may glisten,
  Faith is strong, and hope is free,
But mortal ear no more shall listen
  To the song that rules the sea.

When the grey-haired sailor chaunted,
  Every wind was hushed to sleep—
Like a virgin bosom panted
  All the wide reposing deep.

Bright in beauty rose the star-fish
  From her green cave down below—
Right above the eagle poised him—
  Holy music charmed them so.

'Stately galley! glorious galley!
  God hath poured his grace on thee!
Thou alone mayst scorn the perils
  Of the dread devouring sea!

'False Almeria's reefs and shallows,
  Black Gibraltar's giant rocks,
Sound and sand-bank, gulf and whirlpool,
  All—my glorious galley mocks!'

'For the sake of God, our maker!—
  (Count Arnaldos' cry was strong)—
'Old man, let me be partaker
  In the secret of thy song!'

'Count Arnaldos! Count Arnaldos!
  Hearts I read and thoughts I know;
Wouldst thou learn the ocean secret,
  In our galley thou must go.'

SONG FOR THE MORNING OF ST. JOHN THE BAPTIST.

———◆———

[THE Marquis du Palmy said many years ago in his ingenious essay *Su la vie privée des François*—'Les feux de la Saint Jean, fondés sur ce qu'o lit dans le Nouveaux Testament (St. Luc. i. 14,) que les nations se rejouirer a la naissance de Saint Jean, sont presque steints par tout.'

Both in the northern and the southern parts of Europe there prevailed of ol a superstitious custom, of which the traces probably linger to this day in man simple districts. The young women rose on this sacred morning ere the su was up, and collected garlands of flowers, which they bound upon thei heads ; and according as the dew remained upon these a longer or a shorte time, they augured more or less favourably of the constancy of their lovers Another ceremony was to enclose a wether in a hut of heath, and dance an sing round it, while she who desired to have her fortune told stood by the door If the wether remained still, the omen was good. If he pushed his horn through the frail roof or door, then the lover was false-hearted.

That the day of the Baptist was a great festival among the Spanish Moor the reader may gather from many passages in the foregoing ballads, particu larly that of The Admiral Guarinos. There are two in the Cancionero whicl show that some part at least of the amorous superstitions of the day were als shared by them. One begins—

> La mañana de San Juan, salen a coger guirnaldas
> Zara, muger del Rey Chico, con sus mas queridas damas.

The other—

> La mañana de San Juan, a punta que alboreava,
> Gran fiesta hazen los Moros por la vega de Granada,
> Rebolviendo sus cavallos, y jugando con las lanças,
> Ricos pendones en ellas, labrados por las amadas.
> *El moro que amores tiene, señales dellos monstrava,*
> *Y el que amiga no tenia, alli no escarramuçava, &a.*

Come forth, come forth, my maidens, 'tis the day of good St. John,
It is the Baptist's morning that breaks the hills upon ;
And let us all go forth together, while the blessed day is new,
To dress with flowers the snow-white wether, ere the sun has dried the dew.

Come forth, come forth, &c.

Come forth, come forth, my maidens, the woodlands all are green,
And the little birds are singing the opening leaves between ;
And let us all go forth together, to gather trefoil by the stream,
Ere the face of Guidalquiver glows beneath the strengthening beam.

Come forth, come forth, &c.

Come forth, come forth, my maidens, and slumber not away
The blessed blessed morning of the holy Baptist's day ;
There's trefoil on the meadow, and lilies on the lee,
And hawthorn blossoms on the bush, which you must pluck with me.

Come forth, come forth, my maidens, the air is calm and cool,
And the violet blue far down ye'll view, reflected in the pool ;
The violets and the roses, and the jasmines all together,
We'll bind in garlands on the brow of the strong and lovely wether.

Come forth, come forth, my maidens, we'll gather myrtle boughs,
And we shall learn from the dews of the fern, if our lads will keep their
    vows :
If the wether be still, as we dance on the hill, and the dew hangs sweet on
    the flowers,
Then we'll kiss off the dew, for our lovers are true, and the Baptist's blessing
    is ours.

JULIANA

Page 113.

Come forth, come forth, my maidens, 'tis the day of good St. John,
It is the Baptist's morning that breaks the hills upon;
And let us all go forth together, while the blessed day is new,
To dress with flowers the snow-white wether, ere the sun has dried the dew.

JULIANA.

[THE following ballad is inserted in this place on account of an allusion it contains to the ancient custom which forms the subject of the preceding one. It seems to represent the irenzy of a Spanish knight, who has gone mad, in consequence of his mistress having been carried off in the course of a Moorish foray.]

' OFF! off! ye hounds!—in madness an ill death be your doom!
The boar he killed on Thursday on Friday ye consume!
Ay me! and it is now seven years I in this valley go;
Barefoot I wander, and the blood from out my nails doth flow.

' I eat the raw flesh of the boar—I drink his red blood here,
Seeking, with heavy heart and sore, my princess and my dear:
'Twas on the Baptist's morning the Moors my princess found,
While she was gathering roses upon her father's ground.'

Fair Juliana heard his voice where by the Moor she lay,
Even in the Moor's encircling arms she heard what he did say;
The lady listened, and she wept within that guarded place—
While her Moor lord beside her slept, the tears fell on his face.

I

THE SONG OF THE GALLEY

[CANCIONERO of Valencia, 1511 :
Galeristas de España
Parad los remos, &c.]

Ye mariners of Spain,
  Bend strongly on your oars,
And bring my love again,
  For he lies among the Moors !

Ye galleys fairly built
  Like castles on the sea,
Oh, great will be your guilt,
  If ye bring him not to me.

The wind is blowing strong,
  The breeze will aid your oars ;
Oh, swiftly fly along—
  For he lies among the Moors !

The sweet breeze of the sea
  Cools every cheek but mine ;
Hot is its breath to me,
  As I gaze upon the brine.

Lift up, lift up your sail,
  And bend upon your oars ;
Oh, lose not the fair gale,
  For he lies among the Moors !

It is a narrow strait,
  I see the blue hills over ;
Your coming I'll await,
  And thank you for my lover.

To Mary I will pray,
   While ye bend upon your oars ;
'Twill be a blessed day,
   If ye fetch him from the Moors !

THE WANDERING KNIGHT'S SONG.

[IN the Cancionero of Antwerp, 1555 ·
   Mis arreos son las armas
   Mi descanso el pelear.]

My ornaments are arms,
   My pastime is in war,
My bed is cold upon the wold,
   My lamp yon star :

My journeyings are long,
   My slumbers short and broken ;
From hill to hill I wander still,
   Kissing thy token.

I ride from land to land,
　　I sail from sea to sea—
Some day more kind I fate may find,
　　Some night kiss thee !

SERENADE.

[FROM the Romancero General of 1604.
Miontras duerme mi niña, &c.]

WHILE my lady sleepeth,
　　The dark blue heaven is bright—
Soft the moonbeam creepeth
　　Round her bower all night.
Thou gentle, gentle breeze !
　　While my lady slumbers,
Waft lightly through the trees
　　Echoes of my numbers,
Her dreaming ear to please.

Should ye, breathing numbers
　　That for her I weave,
Should ye break her slumbers,
　　All my soul would grieve.
Rise on the gentle breeze,
　　And gain her lattice' height
O'er yon poplar trees—
　　But be your echoes light
As hum of distant bees.

All the stars are glowing
  In the gorgeous sky ;
In the stream scarce flowing
  Mimic lustres lie :
Blow, gentle, gentle breeze !
  But bring no cloud to hide
Their dear resplendencies ;
  Nor chase from Zara's side
Dreams bright and pure as these.

THE CAPTIVE KNIGHT AND THE BLACKBIRD.

[CANCIONERO of Antwerp, 1555.]

'Tis now, they say, the month of May—'tis now the moons are bright ;
'Tis now the maids, 'mong greenwood shades, sit with their loves by night
'Tis now the hearts of lovers true are glad the groves among ;
'Tis now they sit the long night through, and list the thrush's song.

' Woe dwells with me, in spite of thee, thou gladsome month of May !
I cannot see what stars there be, I know not night from day ;
There was a bird, whose voice I heard—oh ! sweet my small bird sung—
I heard its tune when night was gone, and up the morning sprung.

' To comfort me in darkness bound, comes now no voice of cheer ;
Long have I listened for the sound, there is no bird to hear :
Sweet bird ! he had a cruel heart whose steel thy bosom tore ;
A ruffian hand discharged the dart that makes thee sing no more.

' I am the vassal of my King—it never shall be said
That I even *hence* a curse could fling against my liege's head ;
But if the jailer slew the merle, no sin is in my word,—
God, look in anger on the churl that harmed my harmless bird !

'Oh, should some kindly Christian bring another bird to me,
Thy tune I in his ear would sing, till he could sing like thee;
But were a dove within my choice, my song would soon be o'er,
For he would understand my voice, and fly to Leonore.

'He would fly swiftly through the air, and though he could not speak,
He'd ask a file, which he could bear within his little beak;
Had I a file, these fetters vile I from my wrist would break,
And see right soon the fair May moon shine on my lady's cheek'

It chanced while a poor captive knight, within yon dungeon strong,
Lamented thus the arrow's flight that stopped his blackbird's song,
(Unknown to him) the King was near; he heard him through the wall;
'Nay, since he has no merle to hear, 'tis time his fetters fall.'

VALLADOLID.

Page 110

VALLADOLID.

[Sepulveda's collection, Antwerp, 1580.

En los tempos que me vi, &c.]

My heart was happy when I turned from Burgos to Valladolid;
My heart that day was light and gay—it bounded like a kid.
I met a Palmer on the way—my horse he bade me rein:
'I left Valladolid to-day—I bring thee news of pain—
The lady-love whom thou dost seek in gladness and in cheer,
Closed is her eye, and cold her cheek: I saw her on her bier—

'The priests went singing of the mass—my voice their song did aid;
A hundred knights with them aid pass to the burial of the maid;
And damsels fair went weeping there, and many a one did say,
Poor cavalier! he is not here—'tis well he's far away.'—
I fell when thus I heard him speak—upon the dust I lay;
I thought my heart would surely break—I wept for half a day.

When evening came I rose again, the Palmer held my steed;
And swiftly rode I o'er the plain to dark Valladolid.
I came unto the sepulchre where they my love had laid—
I bowed me down beside the bier, and there my moan I made:
'Oh, take me, take me to thy bed, I fain would sleep with thee!
My love is dead, my hope is fled—there is no joy for me.'

I heard a sweet voice from the tomb—I heard her voice so clear.—
' Rise up, rise up, my knightly love! thy weeping well I hear ;
Rise up and leave this darksome place—it is no place for thee—
God yet will send thee helpful grace in love and chivalry ;
Though in the grave my bed I have—for thee my heart is sore :
'Twill ease my heart if thou depart—thy peace may God restore!'

DRAGUT, THE CORSAIR.

[THIS celebrated corsair became ultimately High Admiral of the Turkish fleet,
and was slain at the great siege of Malta, A.D. 1565.]

Oh, swiftly, very swiftly, they up the Straits have gone—
Oh, swiftly flies the corsair, and swift the cross comes on ;
The cross upon yon banner, that streams unto the breeze,
It is the sign of victory—the cross of the Maltese.

' Row, row, my slaves,' quoth Dragut—' the Knights, the Knights are
     near—
Row, row, my slaves, row swiftly—the starlight is too clear :
The stars they are too bright, and he that means us well,
He harms us when he trims his light—yon Moorish sentinel.'

There came a wreath of smoke from out a culverine,
The corsair's poop it broke, and it sunk into the brine :
Down Moor and fettered Christian went beneath the billows' roar,
But hell had work for Dragut yet, and he swam safe ashore.

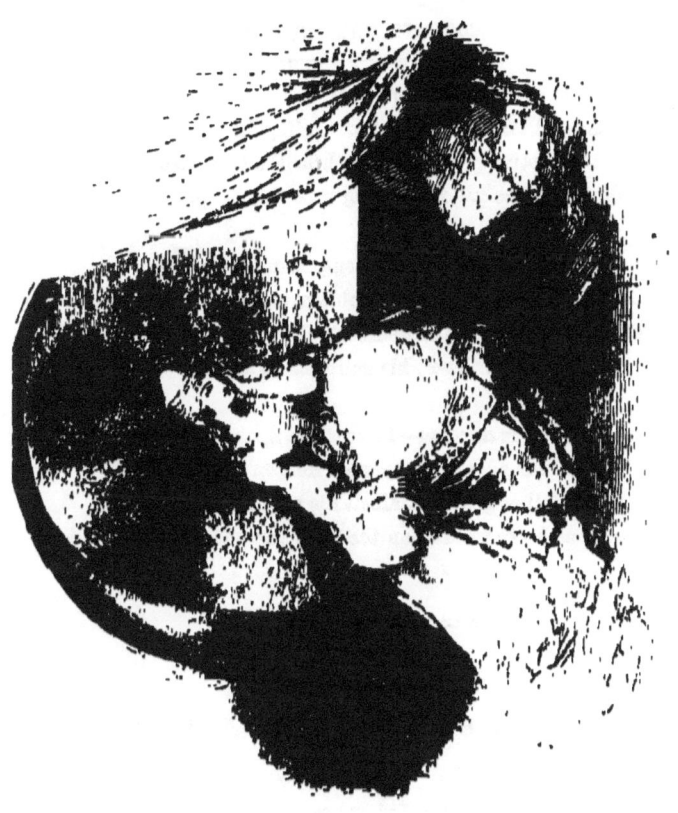

THE INFANTA MARIA

P. 181

One only of the captives, a happy man is he—
The Christian sailors see him, yet struggling in the sea;
They hear the captive praying—they hear the Christian tongue—
And swiftly from the galley a saving rope was flung.

It was a Spanish knight, who had long been in Algiers,
From ladies high descended, and noble cavaliers;
But forced, for a season, a false Moor's slave to be—
Upon the shore his gardener, his galley-slave at sea.

But now his heart is dancing—he sees the Spanish land,
And all his friends advancing to meet him on the strand;
His heart was full of gladness, albeit his eyes ran o'er—
For he wept as he stopped upon the Christian shore.

COUNT ALARCOS AND THE INFANTA SOLISA.

[MR. BOUTERWEK has analysed this ballad, and commented upon it at some length, in his history of Spanish Literature—Book I., Section I. He bestows particular praise upon that line of the thirty-first stanza:—

Dulos me aça este hijo amamaro por despedida.

'What modern poet,' says he, 'would have dared to imagine that trait, at once so natural and so touching?' Bouterwek seems to be of opinion that the story had been taken from some prose romance of chivalry; but I have not been able to find any trace of it.]

Alone, as was her wont, she sate—within her bower alone;
Alone and very desolate Solisa made her moan,
Lamenting for her flower of life, that it should pass away,
And she be never wooed to wife, nor see a bridal day.

Thus said the sad Infanta—'I will not hide my grief,
I'll tell my father of my wrong, and he will yield relief.'
The King, when he beheld her near, 'Alas! my child,' said he.
'What means this melancholy cheer?—reveal thy grief to me.'

'Good King,' she said, 'my mother was buried long ago—
She left me to thy keeping, none else my grief shall know;
I fain would have a husband, 'tis time that I should wed;
Forgive the words I utter, with mickle shame they're said.'

'Twas thus the King made answer—'This fault is none of mine—
You to the Prince of Hungary your ear would not incline;
Yet round us here where lives your peer?—nay, name him if you can ·
Except the Count Alarcos, and he's a married man.'

'Ask Count Alarcos, if of yore his word he did not plight
To be my husband evermore, and love me day and night;
If he has bound him in new vows, old oaths he cannot break:
Alas! I've lost a loyal spouse, for a false lover's sake.'

The good King sate confounded in silence for some space—
At length he made his answer, with very troubled face:
'It was not thus your mother gave counsel you should do;
You've done much wrong, my daughter; we're shamed, both I and you

'If it be true that you have said, our honour's lost and gone—
And while the Countess is in life, remeed for us is none:
Though justice were upon our side, ill-talkers would not spare—
Speak, daughter, for your mother's dead, whose counsel eased my care.

'How can I give you counsel?—but little wit have I—
But certes Count Alarcos may make this Countess die:
Let it be noised that sickness cut short her tender life,
And then let Count Alarcos come and ask me for his wife.

COUNT ALARCOS AND THE INFANTA SOLISA.

What passed between us long ago, of that be nothing said ;
Thus none shall our dishonour know—in honour I shall wed.'

The Count was standing with his friends—thus in the midst he spake ·
' What fools be men !—what boots our pain for comely woman's sake !
I loved a fair one long ago ;—though I'm a married man,
Sad memory I can ne'er forego, how life and love began.'

While yet the Count was speaking, the good King came full near ;
He made his salutation with very courteous cheer.
' Come hither, Count Alarcos, and dine with me this day,
For I have something secret, I in your ear must say.'

The King came from the chapel, when he had heard the mass ;
With him the Count Alarcos did to his chamber pass ;
Full nobly were they served there, by pages many a one ;
When all were gone, and they alone, 'twas thus the King begun :—

' What news be these, Alarcos, that you your word did plight
To be a husband to my child, and love her day and night ?
If more between you there did pass, yourself may know the truth—
But shamed is my gray head—alas !—and scorned Solisa's youth.

' I have a heavy word to speak—a lady fair doth lie
Within my daughter's rightful place—and certes ! she must die.
Let it be noised that sickness cut short her tender life,
Then come and woo my daughter, and she shall be your wife :
What passed between you long ago, of that be nothing said—
Thus none shall my dishonour know—in honour you shall wed.'

Thus spake the Count Alarcos—' The truth I'll not deny,
I to the Infanta gave my troth, and broke it shamefully ;
I feared my King would ne'er consent to give me his fair daughter ;
But, oh ! spare her that's innocent—avoid that sinful slaughter.'

'She dies! she dies!' the King replies;—'from thine own sin it springs,
If guiltless blood must wash the blot which stains the blood of kings :
Ere morning dawn her life must end, and thine must be the deed—
Else thou on shameful block must bend : thereof is no remed.'

'Good King, my hand thou mayst command, else treason blots my name·
I'll take the life of my dear wife—(God ! mine be not the blame !)
Alas ! that young and sinless heart for other's sin should bleed !
Good King, in sorrow I depart.'——'May God your errand speed !

In sorrow he departed—dejectedly he rode
The weary journey from that place unto his own abode ;
He grieved for his fair countess, dear as his life was she ;
Sore grieved he for that lady, and for his children three.

The one was yet an infant upon its mother's breast,
For though it had three nurses, it liked her milk the best ;
The others were young children, that had but little wit,
Hanging about their mother's knee while nursing she did sit.

'Alas !' he said, when he had come within a little space—
'How shall I brook the cheerful look of my kind lady's face ?
To see her coming forth in glee to meet me in my hall,
When she so soon a corpse must be, and I the cause of all !'

Just then he saw her at the door with all her babes appear—
(The little page had run before to tell his lord was near.)
'Now welcome home, my lord, my life !—Alas ! you droop your head :
Tell, Count Alarcos, tell your wife, what makes your eyes so red !'

'I'll tell you all—I'll tell you all : it is not yet the hour ;
We'll sup together in the hall—I'll tell you in your bower.'
The lady brought forth what she had, and down beside him sate ;
He sate beside her pale and sad, but neither drank nor ate.

The children to his side were led—he loved to have them so—
Then on the board he laid his head, and out his tears did flow :
'I fain would sleep—I fain would sleep,' the Count Alarcos said :—
Alas ! be sure, that sleep was none that night within their bed.

They came together to the bower where they were used to rest,
None with them but the little babe that was upon the breast :
The Count had barred the chamber doors—they ne'er were barred till then;
'Unhappy lady,' he began, 'and I most lost of men !'

'Now, speak not so, my noble lord, my husband, and my life !
Unhappy never can she be that is Alarcos' wife.'—
'Alas ! unhappy lady, 'tis but little that you know,
For in that very word you've said is gathered all your woe.

'Long since I loved a lady—long since I oaths did plight,
To be that lady's husband, to love her day and night;
Her father is our lord the King, to him the thing is known,
And now, that I the news should bring ! she claims me for her own.

'Alas ! my love !—alas ! my life !—the right is on their side ;
Ere I had seen your face, sweet wife, she was betrothed my bride !
But, oh ! that I should speak the word—since in her place you lie,
It is the bidding of our Lord that you this night must die.'

'Are these the wages of my love, so lowly and so leal ?
Oh, kill me not, thou noble count, when at thy foot I kneel !
But send me to my father's house, where once I dwelt in glee,
There will I live a lone chaste life, and rear my children three.'

'It may not be—mine oath is strong—ere dawn of day you die !'
'Oh ! well 'tis seen how all alone upon the earth am I ;
My father is an old frail man—my mother's in her grave—
And dead is stout Don Garci—alas ! my brother brave !

' 'Twas at this coward King's command they slew my brother dear,
And now I'm helpless in the land —it is not death I fear,
But loth, loth am I to depart, and leave my children so—
Now let me lay them to my heart, and kiss them ere I go.'

' Kiss him that lies upon thy breast—the rest thou mayst not see.'
' I fain would say an Avé.'   ' Then say it speedily.'
She knelt her down upon her knee : ' Oh, Lord ! behold my case—
Judge not my deeds, but look on me in pity and great grace.'

When she had made her orison, up from her knees she rose—
' Be kind, Alarcos, to our babes, and pray for my repose ;
And now give me my boy once more upon my breast to hold,
That he may drink one farewell drink, before my breast be cold.'

' Why would you waken the poor child ?—you see he is asleep ;
Prepare, dear wife, there is no time, the dawn begins to peep.'
' Now hear me, Count Alarcos ! I give thee pardon free—
I pardon thee for the love's sake wherewith I've loved thee ;

' But *they* have not my pardon, the King and his proud daughter—
The curse of God be on them, for this unchristian slaughter !
I charge them with my dying breath, ere thirty days be gone,
To meet me in the realm of death, and at God's awful throne !'

He drew a kerchief round her neck, he drew it tight and strong,
Until she lay quite stiff and cold her chamber floor along ;
He laid her then within the sheets, and, kneeling by her side,
To God and Mary Mother in misery he cried.

Then called he for his esquires :—oh ! deep was their dismay,
When they into the chamber came, and saw her how she lay :
Thus died she in her innocence, a lady void of wrong—
But God took heed of their offence—His vengeance stayed not long.

www.ingramcontent.com/pod-product-compliance
Lightning Source LLC
Chambersburg PA
CBHW022352020726
47500CB00002B/238